CCS Investigations

Book 4 - DELETED

By

Susan Elle

For

Ursula Publishing UK

DELETED

Book Four : CCS Investigations

Text Copyright © 2014

By Susan Elle

Ursula Publishing UK

All Rights Reserved.

Cover Photograph ©
Dreamstime.com

ISBN   978-1-910753-14-9

Other Books by Susan Elle

The Sara Colson Trilogy
Sara's Child
Sara's Loss
Sara's Shame
All the above also available as audio books.

Catherine Colson-Sayers Investigations
(CCS Investigations)
Book 1 : Missing
Book 2 : The Chosen
Book 3 : Travis
Book 4 : Deleted
Book 5 : Mind Games, due out end Aug 2015, will be twice the length of previous books.

Tempest
Broken

Love, Lies & Consequences Trilogy
Book One : Love
Book Two : Lies
Book Three : Consequences

Langdon Trilogy
Heart & Home
Heart of a Lion
Heart of Stone (coming soon)
http://www.susan-elle.com

TABLE OF CONTENTS

<u>PROLOGUE</u>

The flat was small, dingy and cold, but to Ellen Fisher it was exactly right. It didn't matter that she had to wear a cardigan over a jumper in the winter months, the rent was cheap and no one ever bothered her.

Living on disability benefits for her chronic depression, Ellen rarely stepped out of her front door and had never spoken to any of her neighbours in all the 6 years she'd lived in the Pinewood block of flats.

She was careful not to go out during the day, or when she knew delivery men were about. Ellen had deliberately dropped out of society wanting only to be left alone.

She'd told her stepfather that during the many occasions when he'd forced himself on her. 'Please, leave me alone!' But he hadn't and when she got pregnant he'd told her mother that he'd caught her having sex with a boy in her bedroom.

And she'd believed him instead of me – what kind of mother does that?!

Then there was the humiliation of going to the doctors and sitting there while my mother repeated the story and begged for an abortion for her wayward daughter. What a bloody laugh!

But at least he'd agreed to refer me to a clinic – the thought of keeping 'that man's' baby, feeling the thing growing inside me, was enough to make me go through with something I would never ordinarily have done.

Babies are precious – or so I'd always believed, up to when my mother had met and married Norman Warner.

12 years old, that's all I'd been when he moved into our house and started touching me up. By 13 he was raping me repeatedly until I finally got away at 15.

On the streets I learned to disappear, to live in the shadows and forage for enough food to keep me alive. But it was a living hell. Still, it was better than the life I left behind. Nothing would have made me go back there!

Ellen did everything online, her banking, shopping and even her socialising. She chatted to like-minded people, though she never gave out any personal information, and what she did give out was usually made up. After all, who wants to talk to a nobody who lives in a concrete box and has no life to speak of.

It was a meagre existence – barely any existence at all in reality, but Ellen felt safe as long as she was alone.

People meant hurt and aggravation, and she'd suffered enough of that. At 23, Ellen was young to be such a recluse, but life had taught her some tough lessons in a very short space of time.

Unknown to Ellen she had caught someone's eye and he was watching her – a shadow stalking her life was deleting the few footprints she had left in her wake.

Doctor's records, dental records, even her birth certificate and school records were deleted.

Soon there would be no sign, no record of her existence...and then there would be no Ellen Fisher at all, and who would miss her...?

CHAPTER ONE

The boys were growing rapidly and Catherine was still in awe of the fact that they were hers, that she was a mother, and often had to stop and puzzle out how it had happened.

Watching them play on the sitting room floor and occasionally roll over, Catherine was filled with love and anxiety. Adam and Andrew were a little over 3 months old now, and Catherine had recently changed to bottle feeding her boys in combination with a small amount of baby solids.

Milk alone didn't seem to be enough, so Linda, their honorary grandmother, had suggested introducing a little baby rice and it had worked.

"You're going to be as big as your daddy," she told them with a chuckle. "Imagine the grocery bills. And then there will be another little person in the house soon."

Putting a hand to her stomach, Catherine tried not to frown over the shock of finding out that she was pregnant again.

She had never had a period while breastfeeding the boys and, as Linda had told her that that often happens, Catherine hadn't given it another thought.

But just a few short days ago she had become so sick that Logan had sent for the doctor and he'd given her the 'good news'.

It was taking some time for Catherine to absorb the reality of that revelation. Logan had been overjoyed, hadn't needed to come to terms with any of it.

He amazed her. He'd gone from highly desirable and eligible bachelor to husband and father without so much as a hitch in his stride. Logan was a natural family man and he would love and protect them with everything he has and is.

Even when she'd said, 'Do you realise, we could be the parents of 3 children under the age of 1 – we don't know how far along I am,' Logan had only smiled and said, 'Triplets, just born a ways apart', his smile never faltering.

"Your daddy's a crazy man," she told Andrew as she tickled his belly. "And your mummy must be just as crazy as I think I'm actually getting to like the idea of having another one of you. Maybe we'll give you a sister this time."

Remembering the vision she'd had of a nursery decked out for a little girl, Catherine thought that possibility a very real one. It had been what had caused her to doubt the stenographer's declaration that they were having twin boys – if that were so then why the vision of a girl's nursery. But maybe that had been a foretelling of what would eventually be and not what was about to be.

Still struggling to come to terms with her so-called 'gift', Catherine tried not to think about it. It had almost cost her her life when she had used all her energy to push herself to become visible to Cherish Wade, a way of distracting the demented woman from killing Caroline, Catherine's identical twin sister.

It had worked, but the price she had almost paid was one reason Catherine was spending so much time with her boys – the thought that she might have left them without a mother still had the power to shake her to the core.

Adam smiled up at his mother as she put her tickling fingers to work on him now. "So, what do you think to having a sister, will you look after her when you get bigger? You better had, little man…" she told Adam, then turned her attentions to Andrew "… and that goes for you too."

When Logan came upon the happy scene, he was

thrilled to see Catherine smiling and apparently happy again. "You're looking very content with life," he observed, taking a seat on the floor beside his wife. "Does this mean you're a little happier about the new baby?"

Turning to him, Catherine hadn't the heart to pretend otherwise and nodded. "What's one more – we already had an instant family, it just came out of the blue and knocked me off-balance for a while."

"But your world has righted again?" Logan asked cautiously.

"Yes," she sighed, and smiled brightly when the boys rolled towards each other and smiled. "See that – they love being together. I think they already sense they're special – a very real part of each other."

"I think you're right," Logan agreed. "They certainly seem very aware of each other. The other day, dad was in here holding Andrew and I walked out of the room while holding Adam, they didn't like that at all – both started crying at exactly the same time."

"And did they stop when they were back together again?" Catherine asked, not entirely surprised by Logan's account of their sons' behaviour.

"They did – in fact they both wore very contented smiles for a while," Logan recalled, somewhat amazed.

"I've had similar things happen," Catherine told him. "They definitely have some kind of proximity radar and they don't like it when one of them moves out of a comfortable range," she continued.

"Hmm, could be problematic when it comes to school – twins are not necessarily put in the same class," Logan observed.

"I shouldn't worry, the school will do whatever gives them an easier life. If that means keeping the boys together, I don't see it being a problem."

Nodding, Logan agreed. "Very calmly reasoned out, I must say. Now all you need to do is put that calm reason to work on another problem – I think we need to get you to the hospital for a scan as quickly as possible. We need to know how far along you are and…," Logan hesitated to speak the words that he knew his wife would balk at, "…and we also need to know if you're carrying twins again."

He watched her pale, the smile he loved fading as the unthinkable had been spoken aloud.

"No. I don't even want to think about that possibility," Catherine said firmly. "I've only just gotten used to the idea of being pregnant again so soon, I will not have the thought of another set of twins hanging over me for the next however many months."

Thinking better of pushing her, Logan instead agreed. "Alright, I can understand that. Though, if you think about it, not knowing will have it hanging over you anyway, and there may be only one baby growing in there," he smiled, laying a hand on her almost flat stomach.

She frowned, not liking his logic. "I know what you're doing, Logan Sayers – you think you can wig me out so that I'll agree to the scan, but you're wrong. I'll go when I'm good and ready." But the seed of doubt was already taking hold and Catherine shook it off by picking Andrew up for a cuddle.

When Logan picked Adam up they all went through to the large kitchen, giving Grandma Linda a smile and a wave as they passed her.

"Ah, here they are…" Henry put down his newspaper to greet his grandsons, "…and have they come for their breakfast?"

"Already had it," Catherine told him. "They had an early start this morning."

"Which means you did too," Henry smiled ruefully. "All par for the course when they're this small – but it won't last long, they grow up so quickly you have to wonder where the years went."

Catherine looked at Logan and smiled, then gave the barest hint of a nod. They hadn't told anyone about the new baby as Catherine had wanted time to get used to the idea before everyone bombarded her with best wishes and well-meant advice. But now seemed as good a time as any, and Catherine was giving Logan permission to do what he'd been longing to do since the doctor had made his startling revelation.

"Linda, why don't you join us for a moment..." Logan smiled over at her, "...we have some news to share."

Wiping her hands on a tea towel, Linda frowned and smiled curiously but took a seat at the breakfast table none-the-less.

Taking Catherine's hand, Logan positively beamed. "Dad, Linda, we want you to be the first to know that Catherine is pregnant – we're going to have another baby for you to dote on before very long."

They both looked poleaxed – their eyes naturally turning to Catherine and then dropping their gaze to her stomach as if to see for themselves.

"Well...that's..." Henry shook his head as if to clear his mind. "Well, son, that's quick work is what it is. Are you alright about it, Catherine?" Henry asked with some concern. "I mean, was it planned?"

When Catherine shook her head Linda let out a long sigh. "But you're happy about the pregnancy?"

"I am now," Catherine assured them both. "It was more than a shock when we found out – it's taken me a few days to see the joy in the situation, but it's growing day by day along with our newest member of the family."

"Well..." Henry said again, "...that was quite the bombshell to start the day with, but I'm happy for you.

This house is plenty big enough for a large family – it's what it needs," he declared, his smile now bright as he nodded his head in affirmation.

"I wonder if it will be a girl or a boy," Linda grinned.

"I have a feeling this one is a girl," Catherine said without going into detail. "Just a feeling, but a strong one."

"When are you going to tell the rest of the family?" Henry asked, his eyes now bright with the thought of another grandchild on the way.

"It had better be soon – if your sisters aren't the next to hear they'll both be put out," Logan suggested.

"Too right!" Catherine agreed. "And dad will throw a fit if we don't tell him right after – this family lark is damned tricky."

"But worth it," Logan chuckled, knowing that Catherine was gradually learning to negotiate her way through the tangles that family can throw up.

She had grown up thinking that she was alone in the world, now Catherine has a father, a twin sister and a younger sister to bemuse and bewilder her. But she loves them with all her inexperienced heart.

"Ok, well, I could do with some support when I do impart the happy news," Catherine smiled ruefully at everyone at the breakfast table. "I wonder…how would you feel about filling the house with people over the weekend? I thought, perhaps, a barbecue if the weather holds."

Henry sat back in his seat and smiled, nodding.

"That sounds like a good idea to me," he agreed happily. "This mild weather is sure to disappear soon, we might as well make the most of it while we can."

Looking a little sheepish, Catherine turned to Linda and said, "I know it will mean a lot of extra work for you, but I'll help...if you think I can."

Having never been any kind of a cook, Catherine wasn't surprised when Linda shook her head, and even breathed a very quiet sigh of relief.

"Aida will help me – she loves a good family cookout," Linda smiled, reading Catherine's relief correctly. "Even if the men take care of the barbecue, they'll want accompaniments and puddings, no doubt."

Henry and Logan both agreed with a synchronised, "Of course!" that made everyone laugh.

Spending the next hour with her new family, Catherine enjoyed watching the grandparents enjoying the children. Henry was pulling funny faces at Adam while Linda was cooing sweetly at Andrew, then they swapped babies and continued in the same vein.

"I ought to go up to the office," Catherine said to no one in particular, and not very enthusiastically.

"Have you heard from Emma," Logan asked.

Her partner in Catherine Colson-Sayers Investigations had gone out of town on a case. Emma was doing some field work in the search for a homeless woman who had mysteriously gone missing.

It was a pro-bono case that they had taken on after a Salvation Army person had reported the disappearance to the local police and got no joy.

Their line had been the expected one – *Homeless people go missing all the time, they move on and don't leave a forwarding address because half the time they don't know where they're headed till they get there.*

But the Salvation Army worker had been adamant that this case was different – the police didn't see how and refused to do anything more than keep an eye out for the woman.

The woman, known as Christine, had been on the streets since her mother had passed away 8 years ago. Apparently her death had precipitated a mental breakdown that Christine had never recovered from. She'd left her rented home and all her belongings behind, just put a coat on and started sleeping in shop doorways.

"She called last night," Catherine told him. "It didn't sound very hopeful – I told her not to rush it, to take as long as she needs."

"And you, are you managing your workload ok?" he asked, the concern in his voice not slipping by Catherine.

"Don't worry…" she told him, causing him to do just

that, "…I've got a couple of cases I'm working and another in the pipeline – the rest can wait for Emma."

"The rest – so you are getting a lot of work coming in?" Logan asked, already sure he knew the answer.

"We're doing ok. We should have a good year end figure if we keep up the way we're going."

"And will you be able to do that, even with your pregnancy?"

So, that was the crux of the matter – the issue that was fuelling Logan's sudden concern.

"I worked practically till the day the boys were born," Catherine pointed out, pulling in her natural tendency to get angry when she was being challenged. "I will take rest when I need to and spend time with the boys, and you…" she added quickly, "…as much as I can in between work. You do exactly the same," she pointed out with a raised brow that challenged him right back.

"Maybe so," Logan admitted. "And maybe that is something that will have to change."

"What the hell does that mean?!"

Both Linda and Henry were interested in his answer but were still outwardly playing with the twins.

"It means, financially we are set, there is no actual necessity for either of us to work."

With her jaw dropped, Catherine could only gape at her husband in utter amazement. Where the hell had that come from!

CHAPTER TWO

Looking to his father, Logan took his time in explaining, assessing the man who had first built the business that he had taken over and grown.

"I know it would be hard to let go after all the years of drudgery you put in to building up the firm…" Logan began, watching his father intently, "…but I'd like to sell up, be here full time with my family."

Still not able to find any words, Catherine watched as Henry nodded. "You've always been a grafter yourself…" he reminded Logan, "…I doubt being a house-husband will keep you occupied and fulfilled for long."

"Of course it won't," Catherine finally found her voice and used it to agree with Henry. "You'd go crazy stuck at home all the time – we'd be divorced inside a year!" And, getting to her feet, Catherine began to pace the floor. "You need to think about this. Maybe you've got postnatal depression – it hasn't been that long since the boys were born – maybe it's a late onset, or something," she threw her hands up in the air despairingly.

Chuckling softly, Logan pulled his face into a serious expression when Catherine stopped her pacing to glare at him.

"It's mothers who get postnatal depression," Logan corrected. "And I'm not the least bit depressed – the opposite, in fact. I've never been happier."

"Then you're losing your marbles," Catherine stated firmly. "No one in their right mind would give up what you have to stay home and mind the kids – even your own dad is wondering what's going on in that head of yours!"

Glancing across at his father, Logan could see that she was right. "I'm not losing my mind," he assured Henry, and turned to smile reassuringly at Linda. "I simply don't want to be taken away from home when some trouble or other needs sorting out, and no one else but me will do to fix things."

Only last week, Logan had had to spend 3 days in Birmingham to put one of his branches back in order. As well as the Estate Agency side of the business, Logan had built up a construction crew that specialised in the renovation of old houses and other buildings, but it was all losing the appeal that it had once held for him.

Why was it so improbable that he would be happy to

dedicate more of his time to his family? There were plenty of things to do around the estate, the size of the grounds alone took some upkeep. And then there was the treehouse he'd promised Catherine that he would build, there was so much more to being a father than just changing nappies and helping Catherine to feed the boys.

And then there was his other idea, the one he wasn't quite sure that he should raise right here and now.

As if she had just read his mind, Catherine stopped her pacing and came to an abrupt halt right in front of Logan. "You want in on the investigations business!"

She was looking at him accusingly, not a doubt in her mind that she had guessed correctly.

Well, this hadn't been the way he'd planned to put the idea to her, but it was out now so he would only make matters worse if he denied it.

"I was thinking that we might work together," Logan began cautiously, then watched his father and Linda get to their feet and beat a hasty retreat with the twins. "It wouldn't be such a bad idea, would it?"

She was speechless again — twice in one day was definitely a record.

"I mean, you know I'm pretty good on my computer — I may not have your mad skills, but I can hold my own in a more general way," Logan told her, lifting his chin when she only looked at him with the same scowl.

Pointing a finger at him, Catherine said, "Hah!" like

he'd just stated the one reason why he would be useless at the work. "You know how I work, how Emma works, you would never be able to turn a blind eye to what we need to do to get the job done."

Returning her frown, Logan had to think about that. He hadn't really taken their hacking skills into consideration when contemplating a change in his career.

"I can compromise," he told her. "You don't ask me to learn how to hack into other systems and I won't challenge you when you see the need to do so."

He smiled, pleased with himself for working out a solution to what could have been a sticky problem.

But Catherine wasn't convinced. "Emma and I need to be able to discuss our cases openly, to hash out the information we've gathered and our options for gathering more. We can't do that if you sit in a corner scowling at us for breaking the letter of the law – sometimes we need to work around it!"

Rolling his eyes to the heavens, Logan shook his head. "You steamroller right over it, let's at least be honest about that," he told her, then waved a hand to dismiss his rash statement when her scowl suddenly deepened into a hostile glare. "That's by-the-by," he dismissed. "I don't like it because I prefer my wife to live at home with me and not in some prison cell that her work might earn her. But..." he pushed on when Catherine looked ready to explode, "...I've seen the good you can do with your methods, I won't quibble if you deem it necessary to use them."

Turning to pace again, Catherine was obviously trying to calm herself while giving Logan's proposition some real thought.

But what about Emma, would she be alright with the idea of taking on a new partner – and she could hardly expect Logan to come on board for anything less.

She couldn't make a decision without discussing the prospect with Emma first – Logan surely wouldn't expect her to. Would he?

"I'm not saying yes or no right off the bat," Catherine told him, but continued to pace and think. "I'll need to talk to Emma, get her feelings on the practicalities of us all working together – you'd have to work in the same office," she stated firmly, not willing to compromise in the least on that score. "We'd need to be able to bounce ideas off you – if you come on board you'll need to be as committed to the job as we are. This isn't something you can do just to fill your spare time!"

He stood, then, all his height and build towering over her. "Damn it, Catherine, I hope you know me better than that!"

Not intimidated by him at all, Catherine did, at least, regret the unintentional inference. "I do. You know I do. But we would need to be sure that you're 100% committed – you may end up working out of town like

Emma is right now – that isn't so different to what you do already."

"Ok…" he nodded, giving that some thought, "…then we'll agree that if there is any out of town work to do we'll do it together. Emma can hold the fort here, just as you are doing while she's away."

He had an answer to everything, she noted. But the thought was a good one. The boys would be fine with their grandparents – there could be no better childcare. And if they needed to stay overnight for the sake of the job, at least they would still be together.

Yes, that could work. A man's presence, especially one as imposing as Logan, could even be an advantage. She was beginning to like this idea, had even worked out how she would sell it to Emma.

Turning her face up to Logan, Catherine suddenly smiled. "If Emma agrees, you're on!"

His smile was brief, his lips too busy kissing her. "We'll make a great team," Logan told her, raising his head to smile down at her again. "And Emma likes me, she won't object to me working with you both."

"More than a little bit sure of yourself, aren't you ace," Catherine chuckled and shook her head at his cockiness.

"Just stating my case – Emma's a good sort, I think we'll work well together."

"Hmm," was Catherine's only reply.

CHAPTER THREE

He took Ellen's body away under the cover of an ink black night. The shadow had moved in on her as she returned to her council flat from a visit to a nearby off-licence for a bottle of Vodka, her favourite tipple.

His hand had covered her mouth, stifling any screams she might have made and, with one swift twist of her head, Ellen's neck was broken and her body slumped.

Throwing her into the back of his van, the shadow drove to a wood not 5 miles away. There he took off anything that might identify Ellen — a ring and all her clothing.

Her belongings were meagre; a few coins in a purse and he had no need of that so stuffed it in a black back along with everything else. Then he cut her long tangled hair off and that too was stuffed into the black bag.

"You're nothing!" he sneered at her naked, lifeless

body. "You don't even exist – you're just a blot on humanity that needs to be erased. A user, a sponger – you take, take, take – that's all you've ever been good for. I'm doing you a favour by ending you!"

With that he brought a thick heavy branch down on her head, smashing her face until there was nothing left of it. Then he bent to her hands and used a very sharp penknife to cut off the pads of each finger and even her toes, then they too went into the black bag that contained everything that was Ellen Fisher.

As he'd cut her, the shadow had noticed a tattoo on her arm, just a small dove in flight. Lighting a smaller branch he let it burn for a minute then extinguished the flame and pushed the red hot smouldering end into her flesh.

There wasn't an identifying mark visible on the body and the shadow left her there, his work done for the night. But he'd already begun stalking his next piece of scum.

She was a user too, a nothing, a nobody, a blight on the face of humanity that he would take pleasure in erasing. His work would never end, there would always be more rats in the sewer of life that needed to be exterminated and he would see to it that they were.

When Emma returned to the office a couple of days later, she told Catherine about her progress on the missing woman case.

"Trouble was, I only had her Christian name and very little else to go on – but then I started speaking to a few of the local street people and learned a bit more," Emma smiled, pleased with her work.

"Her full name is Christine Wakelin – I found that out after one of the street people showed me a street where Christine had told him she used to live – though Digger, that's the name he goes by, didn't know whether to believe her or not," Emma continued.

"And I could see why Digger would have doubted her – although they were council houses they were in a really nice neighbourhood," Emma explained while pouring herself and Catherine a mug of coffee.

Handing one of the mugs to her partner, Emma took a seat opposite her and carried on with her story.

"I began knocking on doors, starting at one end of the street and working my way along." She sighed and frowned. "Just my luck to start on the wrong side, and it was a bloody long street, I can tell you. Still, halfway down the other side I got a hit – the old couple had lived there since the beginning of time – they remembered Christine and the way she cared for her mother."

"So, you hit the jackpot – did they have any idea where she might have gone?" Catherine asked.

"No. They didn't think there were any other living

relatives – at least, they never saw anyone else visit the house and Christine had never mentioned anyone. And they'd asked," Emma stated. "They were concerned for Christine. They believed she had some learning difficulties and taking care of an elderly, disabled mother all on her own was hard work. Apparently she did it for years, never complained and asked the neighbours not to mention their worries to Social Services – she was afraid they'd take her mother away from her and into a hospital."

"She was probably right," Catherine agreed, thinking of her childhood and the 'do-gooders' who had interfered in her life, keeping her away from the father who had wanted to take her to live with him after her mother had been murdered. "They always think they know best!"

Watching her partner, and very good friend, Emma felt sorry for the troubled past she knew Catherine had endured, but said nothing. The last thing Catherine would want was her pity.

"Well, the neighbours must have agreed with you because they kept their concerns to themselves, minding the mother when Christine had to go out and helping in any way they could," Emma recalled. "Then they told me the strangest thing. One day Christine was there looking after her mother, the next she was gone."

"What about the mother – surely she didn't just abandon her after caring for the woman all that time?"

"No. When the neighbours didn't get an answer after they knocked on Christine's front door, they called the police, worried that something had happened to her and that the mother wouldn't have anyone to take care of her," Emma explained, blowing out a breath.

"They found the mother already deceased – natural causes according to the police who got back to them on it. But there was never any sign of Christine after that last time – she left the house after her mother died and didn't take a thing with her, as far as the neighbour was able to tell."

"That's rough, did anyone bother to look for her?"

"The neighbours said yes – they kept in touch with the police for quite a while after Christine disappeared but she was never found, apparently."

"So, how come this Salvation Army woman knows all about her – if Christine wanted to disappear I doubt she confided in the woman," Catherine conjectured thoughtfully.

"Major Trumann said she'd gotten to know Christine over the years – she takes out basic supplies to the homeless on a regular basis," Emma informed Catherine. "Though she didn't know how Christine had ended up on the street – she just speculated that Christine had had some sort of breakdown after the death of her mother. All Christine would say was 'mummy's dead – she doesn't need me anymore'.

"So, this Major – hell, what is with that, do they run their church like a real army?" Catherine asked, totally bemused and distracted by the concept

Chuckling softly, Emma tried to explain. "From what I could tell, they see themselves as God's army, bringing salvation to those who seek it and those in need – hence the name, Salvation Army."

Frowning into her coffee, Catherine said, "Well it sounds creepy to me. I mean, what if some Major, or Colonel, gives you an order to do something you don't want to do – do they court-martial you and sentence your soul to some kind of eternal purgatory?" Catherine shuddered, continuing to frown.

Laughing freely now, Emma could only shake her head. When she was able to speak she said, "Trust you to take the idea to its nth degree. I really don't think it works like that at all – they're just a group of Christian people who want to help those in need. The rank stuff is just a way of organising themselves – a level of responsibility, I think, for getting things done. But that's just a guess on my part," Emma admitted.

Giving her head a shake to dislodge the confusion, Catherine went back to the matter in hand.

"Did you go back to Major Trumann and tell her what you'd found out?"

"I did. She wasn't surprised by any of it as it was what she'd supposed all along. But she was glad to have Christine's full name and an old address – I think it made Christine more of a real person in her mind. A lot of street people make up their names, like Digger," Emma said.

"What are you planning to do now?" Catherine asked, leaning back in her seat.

"I'm going to do a few searches, see what I can find online about Christine Wakelin. Then I'll do the usual stuff, medical records, etc."

"If she's got any kind of medical issues Christine may have had to go to another doctor or medical centre to get a prescription or treatment," Catherine suggested. "It might pay to look at other local facilities – or in the general area in case she's just moved on."

"Will do," Emma replied as she got to her feet. Then she turned back to Catherine and said, "Didn't you say you had something to discuss with me – or has whatever it was solved itself?"

Catherine had, indeed, told Emma that they had something to discuss when she got back to the office. But she hadn't wanted to discuss Logan's proposal over the phone.

"Ah, yes, I did didn't I…" Catherine agreed, fidgeting in her seat. "Perhaps you'd better sit down again."

Giving Catherine a lopsided smile and a curious frown,

Emma sat herself back down and watched her partner squirm.

"You look... Heck, I don't really know what you look – should I be nervous?" Emma chuckled, and realised that she was suddenly very nervous.

"No, it's nothing to do with you," Catherine tried to reassure her. "Well, yes, of course it's to do with you it just isn't a bad thing to do with you."

Emma's brows went up in astonished surprise, she had never seen Catherine this flustered. "Spit it out – something has obviously got you rattled."

"I'm not rattled!" Catherine snapped defensively. "I just don't want this to sound like a done deal because it isn't – not unless you agree."

While her partner took a breath Emma said, "Tell me what it is you want me to agree to and I'll give it my undivided attention."

She got to her feet – Catherine always thought better that way. And besides, the chair just wasn't big enough to allow her to 'move'. She paced, and Emma let her without speaking a word – it was obvious, now, that this was important to Catherine.

"You know that Logan had to be away on business last week, right?" Catherine looked at Emma and waited for her to nod. "Well, he didn't like being away from Lakelands – away from the boys," she added, never thinking to include herself in the list of what Logan missed while he was away from home. "He's been talking to his dad – feeling him out about the business he was solely responsible for getting off the ground."

Catherine looked at Emma, her eyes piercing, trying to see if the joint owner of CCS Investigations had cottoned on yet. "Logan wants to sell up – he wants to be at Lakelands full time." She hesitated for only a minute then said, "He wants to work with us."

Her heart was pounding fit to burst and now her lungs were following suit as she held a nervous breath.

"Are you kidding me?" Emma looked shocked and her jaw dropped. "You want Logan to work in here, with us?"

Closing her eyes, Catherine let out the breath she'd been holding in a long sigh of disappointment. She couldn't blame Emma for not wanting the intrusion – all the reasons she'd given Logan for his idea not working were valid ones.

Emma would feel crowded, watched over and inhibited when they did what they did to unearth a lot of deeply buried information.

Why had she ever thought that Emma might agree?

"Oh…my…god…" Emma's eyes were wild, she looked like all her Christmas' and birthdays had come at once. "Does this mean I get to share a desk with Logan?" When she said his name it sounded like a prayer. "I mean, he's going to need somewhere to work, right, and I sure as heck don't mind scooting over to make room for him."

"Will you stop drooling over my husband?!" Catherine was watching Emma virtually melt into a puddle where she sat. "Does this mean you don't object? Or, at least, that you don't object to the basic idea of the suggestion?"

"Are you kidding me?" Emma asked again — only this time Catherine realised that she wasn't saying it in a negative way.

Giving her head a small shake, Catherine gathered up their mugs and swilled them under the tap then moved over to the coffee making area.

She'd taken that time to get her thoughts together — Emma obviously wasn't averse to the idea of Logan working with them — but what about making him a partner?

She couldn't expect Logan to work for anything less. Christ, he was a multi-millionaire, she couldn't offer him a mere office job...could she?

Taking the filled mugs over to her desk, Catherine handed Emma's back to her and retook her seat. For a moment she just stared at her partner then decided to take the bull by the horns.

"I want to offer Logan a share of the partnership." There, she'd said it, and the ceiling hadn't fallen in on her head. "So...what do you think?"

But Emma's reply both surprised and annoyed Catherine. "Well, duh – I didn't think you were talking about him being the new filing clerk! Of course he'll be a partner – I assume you're talking about a 40:30:30 split?"

"You'd be ok with that?" Catherine asked, not sure Emma had given the prospective changes enough serious consideration.

"I'm totally fine with it." Then Emma's expression changed to one of ecstatic glee. "This means we get to initiate him into the business – oh, oh, I'm going to think up something really-"

"No! You're not!" Catherine watched as her friend deflated, a comical look of abject disappointment replacing the glee. "We'll have a small celebration with the rest of the household…" she offered by way of compensation, "…and you can invite your boyfriend – that way you won't devour Logan along with the apple pie."

"But he gets to share my desk, right?" Emma asked, her expression hopeful.

"He can get his own desk, there's plenty of room in here for Logan to have his own workspace." Catherine looked at Emma with a curious frown and asked, "What is wrong with you, is one man not enough?"

"Actually, Sloane is great. He's really coming around to what we do," Emma smiled. "Well, as long as I don't actually tell him what we're doing – that would be like rubbing his nose in it, him being a Detective and all."

"Hah!" Catherine laughed, knowing exactly how Sloane Shivers felt about what they did. His boss, Inspector Frank Harper, was another matter. He did get what they were doing and he often used their 'unique skills' to assist with difficult cases.

CHAPTER FOUR

Having sworn Emma to secrecy over their discussion, not even allowing her to congratulate Logan on joining them, Catherine headed down to confirm the family get together that she'd suggested previously.

"Did you ask Aida if she was up for helping with the barbie?" Catherine asked Linda as she worked on preparing an apple crumble in the kitchen.

Giving Catherine a wide smile, Linda nodded. "She was delighted to be asked, though she would never admit it. But I could tell she was well pleased."

"Phew, well, that's good then, because everyone has accepted the invite," Catherine huffed, glad that everything was going to plan. "Where's Logan?"

"He's out by the lake with his dad, I think," Linda told her, her gaze curious.

"What are they doing?" Catherine was surprised and

wondered what the two men were up to.

"I have no idea – what makes you think they're doing anything but enjoying a walk together?"

"Two men," Catherine stated as though it was an explanation in itself. "Men don't just go out for a walk together, they do it to plan something," she told Linda

But Linda just chuckled. "You've got a suspicious mind, Catherine. I'm sure they're just catching up with each other – Henry loves having you all here."

"He does?" Catherine was pretty sure that they had made the right decision to move to Lakelands, to make it their home, but it was nice to hear that it had made Henry happy too.

"He told me it had been a long held dream of his – that he'd wanted to know that his son's family would continue to care for and live in the home he'd shared with his Ellie," Linda recalled quietly. "He couldn't bear the thought of strangers moving into the house and what they might do to it."

"Has he talked to you about Ellie?" Catherine asked, surprised that Henry had opened up to someone he hadn't known for all that long really.

Understanding the question, Linda nodded and moved to put the kettle on. "I think Henry was glad to have someone that he could talk to about her – I don't think he and Logan do much of that, they both still miss her terribly."

Catherine frowned, should she have realised that Logan needed to talk to someone about his mother. Was she a bad wife for not sensing that about him?

Well, what the hell am I supposed to do, read his damn mind?! Just because I get flashes of…of…whatever the hell I get flashes of…doesn't make me a bloody mind-reader! Logan should tell me if he's upset about something or if he just needs to talk – he knows I don't have any experience of those kinds of things. He bloody well knows that! Now what am I supposed to do?

Watching the worry play across Catherine's face, Linda takes pity on her and suggests they have a nice cup of tea and a few chocolate chip biscuits.

"I always keep some in because I know they're your favourite," Linda smiled kindly.

"Ok. That sounds good," Catherine said distractedly.

"You know, marriage isn't that hard to work out," Linda assured Catherine as she handed her a mug of tea and placed a plate of biscuits on the table between them.

"Huh, easy for you to say," Catherine huffed as she chomped on a biscuit.

Understanding the younger woman's outlook on life, and how it had been shaped by a very disturbing past, Linda took the time to explain. "There's only one golden rule you ever need to remember and it only has one word – kindness," she smiled, and watched Catherine frown in confusion. "I always used to set a goal to carry out at least one act of deliberate kindness towards my husband every day and I was always rewarded with a smile and his love."

Hearing the wistful note in her voice, Catherine felt sorry that Linda had lost 'her Larry' as she so often called him. "You still miss Larry, don't you?"

"That will never change," Linda smiled, her eyes distant with remembering. "Larry was the love of my life – much as Ellie was for Henry. I think that's why he can talk to me about her, he knows I'll understand."

"I'm glad – for both of you. It must be awful to want to share your memories and have no one to do it with."

Catherine understood solitude, she'd courted it almost religiously as she'd been growing up in foster care, and then as a young woman out in the big bad world.

Now she had sisters and a dad, after growing up thinking that she was alone in the world. She'd had no one to share her dreams and ambitions with, and she'd told herself that she didn't care. But now Catherine was beginning to understand what 'family' meant, and also knew that she would do anything to keep and protect it.

"You look sad, Catherine – I didn't mean for you to be, not on my account," Linda told her, covering Catherine's hand with her own.

"I like that," Catherine said, looking at their hands and surprising herself and Linda with her honesty. "I never used to – I couldn't stand anyone touching me, physically or emotionally. But I think I'm starting to get more comfortable with it," she admitted, though her cheeks had lit up like a Belisha beacon.

Giving the hand beneath hers a gentle squeeze, Linda said, "You have a kind heart, Catherine. Now that you've started to let people into it you'll reap the many rewards that trust will bring you. But it won't always be easy – it isn't for all of us that grew up without the tragedy you've had in your life – but for you it will probably be even more difficult. Just try to follow your heart and your natural instincts – kindness is a word that goes a very long way with family too."

Having finished her tea, Catherine got up from the kitchen table and made to leave. Then she smacked a hand to her forehead, causing Linda to grimace at the painful sound of it.

"I almost forgot..." Catherine ducked out of the kitchen and made a quick search of the immediate downstairs area, coming back to Linda with a conspiratorial smile on her face, "...the reason I asked if Logan was about earlier – I want to celebrate a big decision he's made. You probably heard that he wants to give the property business up and come on board with me and Emma?" Linda nodded and Catherine's smile grew brighter. "Well, I discussed it with Emma and she's all for it, but I don't want him to know it's a done deal until the barbie, then I'll surprise him with the partnership papers, making it all official."

"Good job you've only got a couple of days to wait — you look like you could burst with the secret," Linda laughed.

Baby monitors were in most of the downstairs rooms, and now they listened as the twins woke up.

"Bit early for their feed — do you want me to help bring them down to the sitting room?" Linda asked.

"Yes…" Catherine smiled happily, "…I'll get the twin pushchair out and take them for a walk to see their daddy and grandad."

They found Logan and Henry standing by the large lake, looking across the water to the small shack that had been Ellie's art studio.

"The boys were restless so I brought them out to enjoy some of this mild weather we've been lucky to get," Catherine told the two men as they turned and saw her.

Logan felt the familiar swell of his chest at the sight of his lovely wife and children. And wasn't that a thrill. He'd begun to wonder if love would ever happen for him, but when it had he'd fallen as hard as any man could.

"You look so happy," he told Catherine, bending to kiss her smiling lips.

Moving a hand in front of her, she indicated their

surroundings. "We live in the most beautiful place on God's green earth – what's not to be happy with?"

"I'm glad you've settled so well," Henry told her.

"I have," Catherine nodded, and sighed with utter satisfaction at her lot in life. "I love to imagine the boys growing up here. Though, I don't know if Logan has told you, I did think some sort of penned off area might be in order while the boys are very young," Catherine suggested tentatively. "A sort of playground with a swing and a slide in it. And maybe a small sandpit," she added as the idea came to her.

"We've been discussing that very thing," Henry told her. "And a secured playground is exactly what we came up with."

"We thought we'd use a good quality rubber covering for the groundwork – some sort of safety material to give tumbling tots a soft landing," Logan grinned.

"Oh wow. That sounds brilliant. And what about a roundabout – I always loved that when I was little. And a see-saw!" And she snapped her fingers at the 'aha' moment.

Both men chuckled at her enthusiasm and Catherine felt her cheeks heat up. "You think it's too much?"

Logan put his arm across her shoulders and hugged Catherine into his side. "I think it will be just right. Imagine what fun all the nieces and nephews will get out of it."

Brightening, Catherine looked up at her husband with eyes full of love. "That's right. We can make it big enough for them all to play in – I almost can't wait for next summer to enjoy it with them."

"You might be a bit busy for a while there," Logan reminded her, his eyes glancing pointedly at her stomach.

Having put one arm around his waist, Catherine used her free hand to lay it over her belly. "We don't have a date yet," she murmured softly, looking down to where her baby bump would soon become evident. "I suppose we really had better get that scan done."

She didn't feel his sigh of relief, but Catherine did think she felt a lot of tension drain out of him.

"I'll call your doctor and arrange it," Logan told her. "Hopefully we'll get in sometime next week."

"You don't look thrilled at the prospect, Catherine," Henry observed. "Is there something you haven't told us?"

Quickly shaking her head, Catherine gave her father-in-law a warm reassuring smile. "No, it's nothing to worry about – I'm just not sure I want to know if I'm pregnant with twins again." She grimaced. "Can you imagine it – four children under 1 year old?!"

Looking shocked and a little taken aback at the thought, Henry could see her point. "I hadn't thought of it that way – but it won't necessarily be twins. You could be having one baby, right?"

"Whether it's twins or one on its own, we'll get some help in for Linda and manage whatever happens," Logan said firmly. "The main thing is to look after you – you'll need more rest this time, your body hasn't had time to fully recover from the first pregnancy before dealing with this one."

Catherine tilted her head sideways to look up at him, one brow raised. "Have you been looking on the internet again? I swear, he knows more about having babies than I do and I was the one giving birth!" she told Henry, shaking her head in wonder.

"I need to know what's happening, otherwise I won't be able to look after you properly," Logan argued reasonably.

Andrew and Adam had been content to look around at the scenery and listen to their voices, but they were getting restless again and began making their presence known.

"Alright, little man," Logan said as he took Andrew out of the pushchair. "You go to grandad while I get your brother out."

This was more than her heart had ever known to wish for, and Catherine stood watching the two men holding her sons and felt nothing but love and pride.

With a hand to her stomach again, she told her

daughter that it would be her turn soon. *You're going to love your family, and they are going to love you. And when we build the playground, I'll make sure it has a nice Wendy house in it just for you.*

<u>CHAPTER FIVE</u>

Hidden by a privet hedge, the shadow was watching as he had, off and on, for the last couple of weeks. He'd followed her, watched as she'd bought drugs from a dealer and then gone to a regular hangout for vagrants.

There was a metal drum with a fire burning in it, but the druggie didn't bother to huddle round it with the rest. She was too intent on getting her fix, and he watched as she went through the familiar process of shooting up.

Scum of the earth – all of you. But you... he glared at the 20-something bedraggled young woman...*had a good family, there's no excuse for what you've become. You're a leech, you belong in the gutter. You need to be dead and I'm going to take care of that just as soon as I get rid of my other guest! I'd never thought of keeping any of you around, but Christine has been quite entertaining...almost acceptable as far as company goes.*

But you... he glared with disgust and distaste as the druggie lolled back against the wall, the arm she had injected now limp at her side *...when I take you I'll cleanse the world of another taker, delete every sign that you ever existed. You won't infect this world for a moment longer than necessary, and I'm almost ready for you. Almost.*

Catherine had been nervous about the impending family get together, even though it had been her idea. She'd invited Emma and told her that Sloane would be welcome to come with her if she wanted.

"I hope you don't feel you need to invite me just because I live on the estate," Emma had said, not wanting to intrude. "Sloane and I will be quite happy by ourselves. I'm sure we can find something to do to pass the time."

She laughed when Catherine looked embarrassed, aware that her partner was still not comfortable discussing 'personal matters'.

But Catherine had assured Emma that they were both welcome and that she wouldn't have asked if she didn't want them there.

"How's your case coming?" she asked Emma as their Friday workday was coming to an end.

Looking tense and frustrated, Emma looked over her laptop with a deep frown furrowing her brow. "I have her full name, I have her old address, but I can't find a bloody thing on Christine Wakelin. Nothing!" she complained throwing her hands up in the air.

"Why didn't you tell me – I'll give you a hand," Catherine offered, but Emma just narrowed her eyes.

"I can do a standard run. I can even do a deep search into personal records – they just don't appear to exist!"

Knowing that Emma was almost as skilled in computer use as she was, Catherine could understand her friend's annoyance. "Er...just keep me in the loop then."

Realising that she was being petty, Emma shook her head in frustration and said, "If I don't get a hit in the next hour I'll let you know. I really wanted to finish this before the weekend."

And not just because Sloane is staying over. That poor woman has been missing long enough – we need to find out where she is and that she's alright.

But at the end of another hour Emma still hadn't managed to find anything on Christine Wakelin.

"Ok, this is driving me crazy," Emma exclaimed, pushing up from her seat. Striding to the coffee making area, she started making fresh drinks. "If you want to give it a go, you have my blessing. I haven't found a single thing. Not a blessed thing!"

"Make mine a tea," Catherine told Emma. "Use the Lady Grey, it's at the back there."

Then Catherine set to work. She saved her own project and started a run on Emma's.

The first place she looked was The National Archives – she spent a short time confirming Emma's conclusion that Christine Wakelin's records were somehow not accessible. Then Catherine tried the doctor who it is known Christine and her mother were under – again, no records for Christine or her mother, which was out and out strange as the neighbour had confirmed that they used the same surgery.

Deciding to dig deeper, Catherine hacked into the Post Office and 2 local bank's records in search of Christine's finances. Nothing!

"This is not a coincidence," Catherine told Emma without looking away from her laptop screen. "All Christine's records are gone – I've checked every logical source, including hospital records and local libraries. Now I'm going to use my latest computer programme to search for shadows – it'll find any residue bits and bytes and use them to track back to the deleted information and restore it. But it won't be quick…" Catherine looked up at Emma as she placed a mug of tea in front of her, "…and I can't just leave it running – I need to be here to work the programme to get the best results from it."

"When you say it won't be quick, how long do you expect it to take?" Emma asked, looking at Catherine with searching eyes.

"Why…I won't hold you up. I can finish this on my own

– is Sloane coming over?"

But Emma shook her head. "Yes he is, but that isn't the point. You look a bit peaky, maybe you should start that run tomorrow after you've had a good night's sleep?"

"Ordinarily I might do just that, but we've got the whole family coming tomorrow – are you and Sloane still coming over?"

"Yes," Emma confirmed. "Look, I can stay for another couple of hours, just show me the ropes and I'll take a turn at it while you get some time with the boys and get some dinner inside you."

Sitting back in her seat, Catherine looked up at Emma and grinned. "Are you playing mother today?" But when Emma just tilted her head to one side and looked less than amused, Catherine said, "I'm fine. Really. You get off and I'll give this a couple of hours then call it a day."

When Emma still didn't move or speak, Catherine let out a heavy sigh. "Will you just go – I swear, you're even worse than Logan for hovering over me?"

Accepting that she wouldn't budge Catherine by will alone, Emma conceded to her wishes but decided to let Logan in on her concerns before she left for home.

"Fine, I'll go, but if I find out that you've spent the entire evening up here I will be royally pissed!"

Turning on her heels, Emma shut down her laptop, grabbed up her bag and laid her jacket over her arm.

With a hand on the open office door, she turned back to Catherine and narrowed her eyes. "I mean it, Catherine – you really don't look well!"

For heaven's sake, I'm just pregnant – though Emma doesn't know that yet. Still, even when she does I don't want her fussing over me. I've already had twins, it's not like this will be my first time!

She loaded the programme and started it searching, going into the doctor's records first. It was quicker than she'd anticipated, but the initial results were only indicators that records had been deleted, it would take a little longer to collect the data and restore it ready for extraction.

She was still bent over her laptop an hour and a half later when Logan came in search of her.

"You need to finish up, Catherine," he smiled, and saw for himself the shadows that Emma had mentioned to him earlier. "Linda has cooked us a wonderful meal – spaghetti bolognaise with freshly grated parmesan cheese."

She almost drooled, and knew that Logan was perfectly well aware that it was one of her favourite meals.

"Five minutes…" she told him, holding a finger up to signal Logan to wait, "…I can probably leave this to continue on its own for a while, but I will need to come back up to check on it in a bit."

When she finally stood, Logan waited for Catherine to walk over to him then wrapped his arms around her and pulled her in for a hug.

"I miss you even when we're in the same house," he smiled, his cheek resting on the top of her head, his large hand gently rubbing up and down her back. "And after almost a year of marriage, I still have to pinch myself to believe that it's all real." Lifting his head, Logan leaned back just far enough to see her face and his warm smile would have melted even the hardest heart. "My lovely wife, mother to our adorable sons and carrying another child in your womb – I never dreamed that life could be this good, let alone that my life would be."

She blushed, felt awkward and not at all sure what Logan seemed to see in her. "I sometimes think you need glasses and will one day wake up to wonder what you've gotten yourself into. But I do love you, Logan – that much is most definitely true."

He knew she struggled to believe her luck as much as he did, but he also knew that the reasons for the depth of her self-doubt were deep seated and based on the hurt and pain of a terrible past.

He only wanted to love her, to give Catherine the life she so deserved. His hand came up to gently cup her cheek. "I'll never lie to you Catherine, so when I tell you that I love you, that I adore every single thing about you,

you need to believe me or…"

"Or…?" she asked when Logan didn't continue.

"Or I'll have to make it my life's work to prove it to you…starting now…"

His lips were warm and soft and searching, his hands holding her to him until she imagined she might melt right into him. The heat of his body warmed her own, and Catherine couldn't restrain the moan of pleasure that escaped her when his hand began a gentle exploration of her body.

All thought of dinner had slipped away, they were hungry for something much more immediate and primal.

It was often like this – one touch and the spark of want, of need was so quickly lit that it completely took them over.

Suddenly it wasn't gravity holding them to the planet, or air that kept them alive – it was love and pleasure and a need to give those things in ways that couldn't be mistaken for anything else.

When his hand touched her breasts, Logan was pleased to hear her sigh, was always finding new ways to make Catherine tremble.

It was her pleasure that made his all the more satisfying. Lust was an empty, shallow moment without love to give it meaning. And Logan knew he would spend his life loving this woman and would never have his fill of her.

Catherine, his fiery, straight-as-a-dye enigma of a woman, would always leave him wanting more.

Instead of going down for dinner, they took a diversion to the bedroom and sated other appetites first.

"I don't know how you do it, but my body feels glowy and liquid all at the same time," Catherine told him when Logan settled himself beside her.

His breathing was ragged, his heart still pounding from their lovemaking, but he knew exactly what she meant. "You do that to me too, you know."

She leaned up on one elbow to look down into his handsome face and warm brown eyes. "Do I really? But wouldn't it be the same if you did the exact same things with another woman – I mean, men are different, aren't they?" she added quickly when Logan frowned up at her.

"I should whip your arse for that comment," Logan said through pursed lips. "But I'll let it pass because I know you didn't mean it the way it sounded."

He could see that Catherine looked genuinely bemused, then he watched her suck in her bottom lip and start chewing on it nervously.

Letting out a long sigh, Logan put a hand to Catherine's cheek and smiled. "Young men, in general, can be dogs when it comes to sex. We're brought up to think it's ok to go forth and sew our wild oats, and you're right, it doesn't mean much more than a moment's pleasure or youthful triumph."

He could see that Catherine was hanging on his every word, genuinely confused about sex and relationships.

"But you're saying that that kind of transient behaviour stops when young men become adults?" she asked, somewhat sceptical.

"Mostly," Logan conceded. "There are those men who will never be faithful to one woman, who want the thrill of the chase and the triumph over and over again, even after marriage. But I like to think that isn't the norm – that most men cherish the woman they love and treat them accordingly."

He watched as her head tilted to one side as she stared back at him. "But to answer your original question - no, if I did exactly the same things with another woman the feelings and the gratification would not be the same." And he lifted a hand to her cheek, stroking his thumb over it. "It could never be the same because I could never love anyone but you – our love is what makes me want to touch you, to hold you, to fill you and to feel you soar into the stratosphere right along with me when we make love."

She took his lips and brought his lovely speech to an end, holding on to him as if she would never let him go.

He felt her tears as they ran from her eyes and down his face and thanked God for the wonderful, complicated and sometimes belligerent woman he was holding.

CHAPTER SIX

Logan could see that Catherine was excited and nervous about the arrival of so many people that she cared about. She took more care in getting dressed, though a quick swipe of fingers through her growing blonde hair was all the attention she paid to it.

But Logan had to admit, his wife looked really good – but to him she always did.

"Stop fretting," he told Catherine when she asked what time it was yet again. "They'll be here any time now – watching out the window won't make them appear any sooner."

He'd come up behind her, slipped his arms around her waist and pulled her back against his solid frame.

"I can't help it – I don't want anything to go wrong. And you can't let me say the wrong stuff – the last thing I want to do is alienate my family," she said, chewing on her bottom lip as was her habit when she was nervous.

He felt her jump and his arms tightened about her, but Catherine still managed to pull free of him and race to the front door.

Then he saw what she had seen, a couple of cars had turned into the long drive, and he smiled at his wife's childlike exuberance.

She was all but bouncing up and down on the front porch when he joined her, and he took her hand in his to wait for her family to pull up.

They drove to the side of the house and parked, then walked over to embrace their sister, and then him.

"Good to see you all," Logan said to Adrianne and Robert, who was carrying their son Matthew in his baby seat. Then Travis came towards them, a baby seat hanging from each hand, his smile telling Logan that he was proud and happy with that situation. "How are you, Travis – got your hands full, I see?"

"Beautiful, aren't they – and so is their mother," Travis beamed as Caroline came to join them.

"It's a good job I'm not the jealous sort…" Caroline chuckled as she gave Logan a kiss on his cheek, "…Travis has completely lost his heart to the girls."

"I know how he feels…" Logan smiles, understanding the overwhelming love that a father feels for his children, "…but their mother's hold a very special place in our hearts all their own."

"Your husband is a smooth talker," Caroline told Catherine as they walked through to the large sitting room to get settled in.

"What's he been saying?" she asked.

Caroline explained then laughed at Logan's feigned chagrin. "It was a 'men sticking together' kind of thing, I think."

Before anyone can comment further, they turn to the sitting room door as Tom Thornton and Erin Vandivier walk into the room.

"Dad!" Caroline is first to reach him and then Adrianne moves in shyly followed by Catherine.

"Glad to see you all got here alright," Tom told his daughters and nodded a greeting to their husbands. "We're quite the family when we're all together," he smiled, looking around the crowded room.

Five babies and 10 adults were a comfortable fit in the larger than average sitting room, and Catherine was suddenly glad that Logan's family home was big enough to accommodate them all so easily.

"Did you remember to bring swimwear?" Logan asked, looking around the group of adults, and when everyone nodded he smiled brightly. "Good, I thought we could give the babies their first swimming lesson together."

The family chatted and laughed, Henry and Linda took turns holding their grandchildren and asking their parents how each was progressing.

"Sara and Leanne are starting to teeth," Caroline informed them. "Unfortunately when one wakes up so does the other, so night times have been a bit lively of late."

"Sometimes it helps to rub a little bit of whisky on the gums – it acts as a local anaesthetic," Linda explained.

"Alcohol – I'm not sure about that," Caroline frowned uncertainly.

"Just the tip of your little finger dipped into it and then rubbed gently over the gums – for some babies it works really well," Linda smiled.

"How do you know about that?" Catherine asked, overhearing the conversation.

"I was a child psychologist, remember – some of the mothers brought babies along with the older children that I was helping," Linda explained. "They would often talk about their various problems and the remedies they'd discovered."

When Emma and Sloane arrived, Catherine showed them into the sitting room and made the introductions.

Everyone already knew Emma, but a lot hadn't yet met Sloane, her Detective boyfriend.

"Can't imagine you get many weekends off," Henry

said when Sloane took a seat nearby. "Always looks like a 24/7 job when you watch it on the telly."

Sloane nodded, "It can be – though it isn't as exciting as the TV dramas make out. A lot of slog over paperwork at a desk," he added sagely.

Emma managed to side-line Catherine and asked about the case she was working. "Did you get any joy on finding Catherine Wakelin's info?"

"Definitely wiped," Catherine whispered. "But I'm still recovering data and it looks like we might be able to track the action back to the hacker who deleted it all."

Emma's eyes went wide as she listened. "Are you sure? I'd have thought they'd be too clever to leave traces like that? Not just any Joe can do what this hacker did.za"

Smiling not a little smugly, Catherine said, "We're obviously better. And he doesn't know about my latest mining programme so he can't work around it."

The happy chatter continued when they all moved out to the rear patio and the tables and chairs that had been set out.

The men took over the cooking, using the barbecue as if they'd been born to it, while the women settled their babies and waited to be served their lunch.

"I love barbecues…" Caroline chuckled, "…it's the one time we women get to sit back and do nothing."

The rest of the women joined in the laughter and

Emma said, "Sloane can't cook for toffee, but look at him now," and she raised her glass of wine to point in his direction.

And there he was, spatula in hand, turning pork steaks on the grill with one hand while holding a bottle of beer in the other. The men appeared to be taking it in turns, offering tips to the one currently doing the turning and generally congratulating themselves on what a good job they were doing.

Aida wheeled a serving trolley, laden with covered dishes, out onto the patio. "There's mixed salad, boiled potatoes, boiled eggs and grated cheese," she told Henry when he came over to thank her.

"Aida, are you sure you won't stay and join us?" Henry asked, but knew that his housekeeper wouldn't change her mind.

"No, no, I've got a lot of things to do," Aida said as she busied herself putting serving spoons and forks into each dish. "I've given Linda instructions for the pudding – she'll take things from here."

Then the formidable Aida wished everyone a good day and took herself off to the kitchen to clear away before leaving for the day.

"I've known that woman for years but she won't bend," Henry tells everyone. "Seems to think the hired help shouldn't sit at the same table as those who pay their wages – at least, that's more or less what she's told me when I've tried to lessen the formality of our arrangement."

Nodding, Linda turned to Henry and said, "I can understand why Aida might feel that way – I felt that way myself until very recently."

Taken aback, Henry raised his brows. "Well, this isn't the 19th century and slavery went out long ago, thank Christ!"

Deciding not to argue the point, Linda just said, "Not every domestic employer is so enlightened, and not every situation allows them to be."

Henry huffed, picked up a bottle of white wine and offered to refill Linda's glass. "It's just lunch – the woman has to eat, doesn't she?!"

"Thank you, Henry," Linda smiled and took a sip of the chilled wine.

"Better start getting your plates ready, the meats almost done," Henry told them before returning to the men still gathered around the barbecue.

The women gathered around the trolley that Aida had left and filled a plate for their partners, then one for themselves, and took them back to the tables to wait for the men to serve up the meat.

Catherine was quite impressed by their efforts, she was no cook and doubted she could have done as well.

"This is good," she told Logan as she swallowed down a tasty piece of pork steak.

"It should be, I cooked it especially for you." He winked and smiled when Catherine looked up at him not sure if he was being serious.

"Oh really. Well...then I suppose you deserve a reward," and she looked at Emma and gave her a smile. "Be back in a minute."

Logan looked around the family for a clue as to what was going on, and when his eyes rested on Emma she just shrugged and chuckled.

When Catherine reappeared she looked excited but sort of shy. "First, Logan and I have some very special news to tell you all," and Catherine held out a hand to her husband for him to come and join her.

When he was stood at her side, holding her hand, Catherine gave him the nod.

He looked at Tom and Erin, then around the tables to include everyone in his proud smile and said, "We wanted to let you all know together that Andrew and Adam are going to have a little brother or sister. We're pregnant!"

Tom looked shocked and didn't make a sound, Adrianne let out a scream of excitement then shot out of her seat to give them both a hug and shortly after everyone else followed suit.

It took a while for all the congratulations and hugs to

be exchanged, by which time Catherine had forgotten about her other surprise.

"Err, not to be pushy or anything but…" Logan let the words hang and just raised a brow at Catherine expectantly.

"Oh!" she cried in sudden shock, then jumped up to get the manila folder she'd put down before the baby announcement.

Remaining standing, Catherine looked around her family and friends then said, "Logan has decided that he is selling up his business interests to spend more time with us," and she waved a hand towards the sleeping boys in their bouncy chairs.

A round of questions and more congratulations were exchanged then Catherine added, "I just don't see that it would be fair to let my husband go to seed," and she laughed when Logan turned a frown on her.

"So I found him a job that will keep his brain in shape and the rugby will have to take care of the rest."

Everyone gave a laugh and Caroline handed Logan the manila folder that she was holding saying, "Welcome on board…partner."

His jaw dropped and Logan looked from Catherine to Emma, who grinned and held up her wine as a toast

"I never expected this," Logan gasped, struggling for words. "Are you really sure about this?" His brown eyes looked uncertain and anxious, yet lurking in their depths was a flicker of excitement.

"What do you say Emma, are we sure?" Catherine asked with a raised brow already knowing the answer she would get.

"Are we sure…? Hell yes! And I already offered to share my desk with you," Emma grinned, and got an elbow in her side from Sloane.

"Won't it take some time to sell the business?" Tom asked when the joking around settled down.

Nodding, Logan took a sip of his wine and then explained. "I've already had a very decent offer from a competitor for the estate agency side of things – he wants to keep the name and run it alongside his own company."

"Is that usual?" Tom frowned.

"It isn't unusual – it's all about branding and the Sayers Estate Agents have been around for over 35 years." Logan gave his father a proud smile and raised his glass to him.

"What is the other side of your business?" Erin asked intrigued.

"Other side…?" Logan frowned, then it dawned on him. "Ah, I see what you mean – the construction and renovation company. It started out very small, just turning over old properties by renovating and selling them. I often bought from property auctions, ripped everything out and remodelled them to suit whatever market they fit into."

"Do you still do that?" Tom wanted to know.

Chuckling at the thought, Logan shook his head. "One of our latest projects was the renovation of some old factories that we turned into a sizeable shopping centre. We take on a variety of projects, though often it's a disused factory or office block that we turn into loft style flats. Very trendy and saleable."

"Sounds big," Sloane interjected. "Won't that make it difficult to sell – there's a lot of building companies out there already?"

"True, and not all of them are doing well," Logan conceded. "But my crew are very experienced and good at what they do. Reputation is everything and we get a lot of word-of-mouth referrals, especially from large houses looking to renovate a few rooms or build an extension."

"Sounds like you're not short of work," Sloane nodded with some admiration. "Won't you miss it?"

Shaking his head, Logan looked at Catherine and then to his boys. "My life is very different now to what it was when I set the refurb' business up. I was a workaholic – I admit it – I don't remember ever waking up and dreading going in to work. Either I was keeping an eye on the estate agency, troubleshooting any problems there, or I was overseeing the refurbishments and growing the building side of it." He looked sad for a brief moment, then turned his head to smile at Catherine.

"Lately, I've done nothing but dread going to work, even though I can do a lot of the necessary office work from home – I resent it coming between me and my family."

CHAPTER SEVEN

Christine was confused, her hands and feet were bound and there was something over her mouth.

It was dark and cold, but she could see someone moving about. *Is it him, the one who brought me here? Why doesn't he talk to me, maybe he'd like me if he talked to me?* But hard as she tried, Christine couldn't get him to notice her – it was like she didn't exist.

I wonder if Digger is missing me – I like Digger, he helps me and stops the others from bullying me. I bet that's what it's like to have a big brother – I've never had a brother, or a sister, or anyone really. I wish mummy was here – I want to go home…but I don't think I can…something happened…something bad…I don't remember…

A hand reached down and ripped off the tape covering Christine's mouth and she gasped at the pain it caused. "That hurt!" she told him, her eyes frowning up at him, her mouth turned down into a childish pout.

She didn't seem to be afraid of him, and that surprised the man. He stood watching her, not sure why he hadn't already done to her what he'd done to the others. There was something about her that was different, he just wanted a little more time to find out what it was.

"You hungry?!" he snapped out.

She nodded, her cheek scraping on the hard cold floor. "And thirsty," Christine added softly. When he didn't shout or hit her, she got a little braver. "I need the toilet, my stomach hurts."

He watched her for a minute, then said, "You gonna give me any trouble?"

Shaking her head, Christine smiled, "I'm a good girl, my mummy said so."

He thought that was a weird thing to say, but didn't comment. Getting a knife out of a drawer, he cut the tape that bound her ankles and hauled her to her feet.

"You try to run away and I'll tie you up good!" he told her as he guided Christine out the back door to the outside loo. He was still holding the small vegetable knife and held it close to her neck when Christine moved past him. "I'll be waiting right here…" he told her, giving her a warning look, "…so don't you try anything. And keep your mouth shut!"

His voice was low and threatening, his manner dangerous and menacing, yet Christine just smiled.

"You need to cut these – I can't do my knickers else." And turning, she edged closer to him and waited for the binding round her wrists to be cut.

"You better not be trying anything on," he warned. "I can do a lot of damage with a knife like this."

"Oh, I won't take long, promise," Christine smiled, as though all he'd done was get a little impatient.

Her attitude confused him and he stared at the closed door as he listened to her singing. *What the hell?!*

When he heard the toilet flush, the man moved back a little and waited for Christine to emerge. When she did, he grabbed an arm and dragged her back into the house.

There were no lights on, but the man seemed to know exactly where he was going and pulled a chair out for her to sit at a small wooden table.

"You sit right there and don't move, you hear me?"

Nodding, Christine smiled and clasped her hands together in her lap.

Only when the man opened the fridge door did any light spill into the kitchen. But as the man had his head in the fridge, Christine still didn't get to see what he looked like.

He got out a chunk of cheese, a tub of marge and what was left of a loaf of bread. Then he made them both a sandwich and sat opposite Christine while they ate.

"Why are you smiling?!" he barked out, squirrelling a mouthful of sandwich into a cheek. "Damn it, you're always smiling!"

"I like smiling," she replied simply. "I like it here – it isn't as cold as my other place."

He knew where her 'other place' was, he'd watched her for a while, longer than he usually did with those he was working on. He'd already deleted all of her records, the only thing left to delete was the woman herself. Yet he'd brought her back to this house, the place where he did all his computer work, and he didn't really know why.

"So why live in your other place – you must have had a home in the past?"

He didn't know why he was interested, but he was.

"Oh I looked after everything," Christine said proudly. "I used to cook and clean and look after mummy," her smile slipped and Christine looked sad and confused. "Mummy said I was doing a good job, but I couldn't make her better."

"She died?"

He watched as Christine nodded. "I couldn't stay there after that – I knew people would come and take her away, then they'd blame me because I didn't look after her enough. I tried my best, but I think I must have done something wrong...I couldn't wake her up...she got really cold and I couldn't wake her up."

An unfamiliar feeling tugged at his shrivelled heart and he found himself offering some comfort. "Might not have been your fault at all – might be her illness was too bad and she died from it."

"You're nice." Christine's guileless statement surprised him, and the man sat back in his chair to regard her. "You brought me here out of the cold and you don't call me stupid. Digger said only idiots call me that because they don't know me very well."

"Who's Digger?"

"He looks after me – I like Digger."

The man got up and poured them both a glass of milk. "How long have you lived on the streets?"

Taking the glass he held out to her, Christine thanked him and said, "A long time, I think. I don't remember."

For a long moment the man sat looking at Christine, deciding what to do with her. It was time for him to go out again – he had work to do!

"You wanna stay here?" he asked gruffly.

Her smile was bright and Christine nodded quickly.

"Then you gotta do as you're told! You stay indoors and you don't speak to anyone – got it?!"

He got his duffle bag ready then told Christine to sit in an old armchair. "I've gotta put this back on," he told her, picking up a roll of silver tape. "It's to keep you safe," he lied, and bound her ankles together then leaned her forward and told her to put her hands behind her back and did the same to her wrists. But when he tore a strip off and went to put it over her mouth she shook her head and her eyes pleaded with him.

"I won't talk to anyone, I promise. I'll sit nice and quiet, just like you said." Her bottom lip started to tremble and she said, "I'll be good. I'm a good girl."

With pursed lips he got to his feet and put the tape back in his duffle. "You better stay quiet, or else!"

The second he stepped out of the house the man melted into the shadows, becoming one with them.

The day had been a busy one, but Catherine couldn't remember when she'd enjoyed herself more. The barbecue had been great, even the stiff-necked Sloane Shivers had mellowed out and seemed to enjoy himself.

He and Logan had shared a few jokes and Catherine had loved watching her husband laugh. He'd been so relaxed, so at ease with everyone. She'd envied him that ability to mingle so effortlessly, she still found it difficult even with her own family.

Blowing out a breath, Catherine got back down to work. She'd slipped off after putting the boys down for the night, sneaking away to her office to check on the programme she'd left running.

Brilliant! Probably going to take another few hours but

it's making more sense now we've got more data. But who would want to do this in the first place?

From what Emma found out, Christine Wakelin was just a woman looking after her housebound mother, I can't believe that would bring her to anyone's attention. And even if it did, what reason would they have to abduct her and erase her records? Assuming both things are connected.

"Here you are…" Logan shook his head at Catherine but was smiling while he did. "I had a feeling I might find you in here."

Looking sheepish, Catherine gave him a smile that was a cross between a smile and a grimace. "I just needed some time out and a little space."

Coming to stand behind her chair, Logan rested his large hands on her shoulders and began kneading them.

"What are you into – doesn't make a lot of sense from what I can see," Logan frowned, trying to interpret the indecipherable data on Catherine's screen.

"I'm using a new programme I wrote – it's retrieving deleted data and also tracking the computer that did the deleting."

"You can do that?" Logan's hands froze on her shoulders and his deep voice was full of concern.

Looking up and over her shoulder at him, Catherine tried to assess his mood. "Don't make me regret making you a partner – this is what I do."

Shaking his head, Logan moved to sit on the edge of her desk, the better to see her. "I'm not criticising, or judging – I'm only concerned that if you can do this 'tracking' maybe someone else can track you right back."

Raising a brow, Catherine just gave him 'the look'.

"I know you're brilliant and I know you're careful – but what if someone equally brilliant followed the breadcrumbs that you are tracking right this minute? Maybe the breadcrumbs were left deliberately, tempting you to follow them and, instead of you feeling his collar, he finds out who and where you are," Logan speculates, his voice gone soft and low. "Maybe he decides to meet his nemesis in the flesh – you'd be an intriguing adversary."

"Stop wigging yourself out. When I use my hacking programme it cleans up those pesky breadcrumbs of data automatically. No one is going to come looking me up," Catherine tells him, patting the back of his hand,

"Alright, I won't nag, but I'm still going to tell you not to let your guard down – getting cocky is as bad as getting stupid."

"Ok, you're not going to let this go so I'll tell you what..." she stood, moved to stand between his knees and looked Logan straight in the eyes, "...how about I take you to bed – I could use an early night and you could use-"

He didn't let her finish, his mouth was on hers letting her know that he already knew what he could use and exactly where he would be using it.

She'd meant to get some more work done, but Logan's hands knew just where to touch her, his mouth tasting the flesh that he was rapidly exposing.

He loved to kiss the pulse in her throat that beat fast and hard beneath his lips. Her skin was hot, giving off a scent that was only Catherine – his Catherine.

Breathing her in he moved lower, was about to take her pebble hard nipple between his teeth when they both heard someone laughing as they came up the stairs.

"Christ!"

Hands moved quickly, pulling clothing back into place and doing up the buttons they had just undone. They heard footsteps move along the landing, then stop outside the office door, and both of them turned to stare at it.

Anxious moments passed then the footsteps continued along the landing and away.

Letting out a joint sigh of relief they looked at each other and laughed like loons.

"Oh my god – if someone had come in just then I swear I would never have dared show my face ever again." Catherine leaned her forehead on Logan's solid chest and thanked her lucky stars that they hadn't.

"Maybe we should go to bed – I think that might be the safest option with the house so full of people," Logan suggested with a wide smile and his eyes still sparkling with supressed laughter.

CHAPTER EIGHT

When Monday came Catherine was pleased to report to Emma that she had been able to retrieve enough of Christine Wakelin's medical file that she could now make sense of it.

"I've printed it off and written the salients on that whiteboard," she said, pointing to the front wall. "Christine appears to have been suffering long term depression – she was taking 200mg Sertraline for three years prior to her mother's death."

Tapping away at her laptop, Emma looked up. "That isn't a medication you can just stop – or it isn't advised that you do. So where has our girl been getting her meds?"

"Maybe she hasn't," Catherine speculated.

"She was on the highest dose – she couldn't just stop taking it after all that time and not feel the consequences," Emma stated.

"Hmm…from what you learned, Christine seems to have had some kind of breakdown – maybe it was exacerbated by the lack of her usual meds" Catherine mused, reading the notes she'd made.

"Just, off topic for a minute…" Emma began, still looking at the whiteboard, "…but, have you come up with any idea why anyone would go to all this trouble? I mean, Christine seems to be a pretty ordinary woman, this level of erasure would take time, dedication and resources. Why bother?"

Shaking her head, Catherine tries to think of something. "Could it be some kind of insurance fraud – did Christine Wakelin have excessive life cover?"

"I couldn't find any insurance policies for her or her mother," Emma replied. "Even if she had them, they're not there now. And who would make the claim if she did have a policy somewhere – if Christine has faked her own death she could hardly come forward to claim the insurance money."

"But there's something in that, what you said about faking her own death – it just got me thinking," Catherine tailed off, her brain going into overdrive.

"According to some sources, 275,000 people go missing each year in the UK alone – that's the equivalent of the population of Plymouth just disappearing, or another way to think of it is 1 person going missing every 2 minutes. I find that disturbing."

"I bet not all of them have their records wiped the way Christine Wakelin did," Emma scowled, not liking the statistics Catherine had related.

"It gets worse," Catherine frowned, watching Emma cross the room to make coffee. "At any one time, there are an estimated 1,000 unidentified bodies lying in the country's mortuaries and hospitals. There are no figures for how many people are given so-called public health funerals, but a straw poll of local authorities suggests they run into the thousands."

Catherine took the steaming mug of coffee that Emma held out to her and continued. "Depending on which country you live in, it might take a while before you get that council burial. There are quite a few where unclaimed and unidentified bodies become the property of the government. That means they can do with them as they like and usually send them for anatomical study in various scientific or medical institutions."

Grimacing over her coffee, Emma said, "Yuk! You're talking about dissection, right?"

Nodding, Catherine sat on the edge of her desk and regarded Emma without speaking for a minute or two, then said, "Have you spoken to Sloane about Christine Wakelin?"

Not sure if she was dropping herself in it, Emma nodded.

"And what was his take?"

"A bit like yours – he just quoted the same missing figures and said it happens more than we like to think. And that street people are transient in a very different way, that their sense of place is also transient – they belong where they feel comfortable for as long as they feel comfortable, and when they don't they up and disappear."

"So, that's probably what he thinks happened to Christine – but did you tell him about the missing files?"

This time Emma shook her head and said, "I wanted to get the full picture, see what your programme was able to retrieve. But I think it might be a good idea to let him and Frank know what we've found out so far."

"I agree. If you hadn't got that call from the Salvation Army worker no one would be wondering where Christine is or what might have happened to her – a murderer's dream, don't you think?"

Catherine and Emma stood regarding each other for a long moment then both slowly nodded, turning their gaze to the whiteboard that detailed what little they knew about Christine Wakelin.

"Ok, Frank, I'll see what I can do to track his computer and let you know what I find when you get here. Yes, after

4 will be fine – have a good day," Catherine finished and put her mobile away.

"Have you made any headway with that?" Emma asked.

"Not much," Catherine grimaced. "He's better than I hoped." And Catherine thought about what Logan had said about another computer wizard being out there – one as good as she was. *You still left a few breadcrumbs – I just need to work on them a while longer!*

While Emma followed up other leads, Catherine went to work on finding the person who had deliberately deleted all trace of Christine Wakelin.

Once she put her mind to it, Catherine was oblivious to everything else. *He might be good but I won't let him be better – I just have to …yes, that's it…and so it begins to unravel. Better run and hide, I'm on your trail now.*

In the library, Logan was discussing a few changes to the house in readiness for Christmas. November had just begun and Christmas would be upon them in no time.

"I'd like to make Catherine's first Christmas at Lakelands really special," Logan told his father. "She still gets flashbacks to her childhood with Caroline and her parents, but they're more painful than enjoyable."

"You want to give her some new memories," Henry intuited correctly.

"Yes – I was lucky enough to have you and mum, and

a good bunch of friends – Catherine's life has been filled with painful partings and nightmares rather than happy memories," Logan recalled. "I want to draw a line under them, I want to give Catherine the life she always deserved and our boys lots of memories to treasure…starting with a huge Christmas party!"

"Ok, son, what did you have in mind?"

"Well…for a start we'll have it catered – I don't want Linda or Aida working their tails off at Christmas."

"Hmm, you do know that Aida lives alone – working here gives her company as well as an income," Henry explained.

"I won't have them slaving over us at Christmas, we just won't tell them that they are guests until the day," Logan grinned conspiratorially. "We'll let them think they're going to help the caterers, then we'll get Catherine's family to help them mingle with the guests."

His father let out a deep chuckle and clapped Logan on his back. "Sounds like you've been giving this some thought – had any about where we're going to hold this party and how big you want to make it?"

"Well…it would be nice to catch up with a few of my old friends, introduce them to Catherine – and no doubt Caroline and Adrianne will have ideas on guests they'd like to celebrate with."

"Hmm," Henry mused again. "This sounds big – we'd

better open up the ballroom – it needs sorting out so the sooner we get started the better."

Logan grinned. "We haven't had that open since before mum died. It'll be nice to see it decked out again."

"Agreed," Henry chuckled again. "Your mother would like that, a family gathering at Christmas."

<u>CHAPTER NINE</u>

"This is good work," Frank said after going over what Catherine and Emma had pinned on the whiteboards, and the written notes on another one. "Did you manage to track the perpetrator?" he asked, turning to look at Catherine.

"He's good – bounces from one city to another and even one country to another – but I'm getting more on him all the time," she assured Frank.

"You seem to have more detail on Christine," Sloane observed, reading the board that had all of her known details itemised on it.

"I told you about the neighbours I spoke to," Emma said, and Sloane nodded in agreement. "Well, they used the same doctor's surgery as Christine and her mother. That gave us somewhere to look for more information on them, but it was all gone – no history of Christine or her mother ever having been patients there."

"Gone – what are we talking about here? Are you sure you got the right doctor's name from the neighbour?" Sloane quizzed Emma, his tone doubtful.

For a brief moment Emma just stared holes in him, then she huffed out a long suffering breath and said, "I'm positive. I also checked for birth records, hospital records, even the local library records – there's nothing. Everything pertaining to the Wakelin's has been erased. They might never have existed, only we know that they did."

"That doesn't make any sense," Sloane frowned over at Emma then pointed up at the whiteboard. "If all the records had been deleted, where did your information come from?"

"Catherine has a programme that can find deleted files – she put a lot of data back together to make it readable, though not in its entirety. Some information was lost," Emma admitted grudgingly.

He turned to frown at Catherine. "Aren't there already programmes that can do that – I'm sure the police computer forensics department uses one?"

Catherine nodded, "Mine is better and picks up other information at the same time – it's that information that will eventually lead me back to the hacker. I'll have his signature and his location – if we're really lucky I might be able to turn the tables on him."

Emma smiled but Sloane only frowned. "What's that supposed to mean?"

"It means she'll be able to knock on his back door and enter his computer," Emma explained with a grin.

"You really think you can do that?" Frank asked, not doubting Catherine's abilities in the least.

"I do – he's good but my programme is the best. I wrote it with just this kind of work in mind."

Logan coughed to hide his chuckle at her immodesty and Catherine turned to frown at him.

Looking extremely sceptical now, Sloane managed to bite back the urge to scoff and voice his disbelief. "Ok...let's say all that is true." He held up a hand when Emma would have jumped in and said, "Just hold on a minute, we need to think this through. If, as you seem to think, all record of the Wakelin's have been erased...why...why would anyone take the considerable time and trouble to do that?"

"I agree, it doesn't make any sense..." Logan put in, then smiled as Catherine turned a sour look on him, "...but I trust the findings. Just because we don't yet know the why of it doesn't make it not so."

"Well, has anyone come up with an idea for the why?" Sloane asked, a brow raised.

Emma and Catherine looked at each other and Logan

said, "What? I know that look, you know something."

"No, not really," Emma hedged. "It's just something we were batting around earlier."

"Murder," Catherine said before Emma could prevaricate further.

"Murder?" Frank asked as if the idea were ludicrous.

"Yes," Catherine affirmed, not the least put off by the inspector's incredulity. "Just think about it – if someone wanted to commit murder it would be an ideal situation to have the victim completely untraceable."

"But Christine Wakelin wasn't untraceable – you not only found a neighbour that knew her but also her last known address," Sloane reminded her.

"Yes, but she's been living on the streets for the past 8 years – it was pure luck that she told one of her street friends about her old house," Catherine told him. "But as far as the proposed abductor was concerned, she had no home and no one who cared about her. Christine was disposable, invisible to a society that would sooner cross the road than look too closely at a filthy homeless person."

Sloane scoffed but Frank was nodding, giving the idea some thought. "Ok, but if he thought she was just another homeless person, how did he know enough to delete all of her identifying files? He'd have had to know her full name for that, and you already said you only had her

Christian name when you began this case," Frank turned to Emma.

"True, and I've been thinking about that," Emma admitted. "I think he stalked her – followed Christine and listened in on her conversations. I don't believe this was a spur of the moment thing – it's too deliberate for that."

Frank and Sloane looked at each other, their unspoken communication a 'cop' thing. Then Frank nodded and Sloane seemed to take a step back.

"You may have something here," Frank conceded, looking at the whiteboard again. "You've got here that Christine Wakelin was known to have learning difficulties and suffered chronic depression, do you believe any of that played into the proposed abductor's choice of victim?"

"Hard to say, but it would have made it easier to lure her away, maybe even get her to take a ride in a car with him," Catherine suggested.

"She could still be alive," Logan put in, and all eyes turned to look at him. "You don't have a body, as far as you're aware. I'm just suggesting that it's a possibility," he shrugged. "A slim one, I grant you, but you can't write Christine off until you know for sure that she's dead."

Emma closed her eyes and sighed. "And the police may have got it right in the first place – Christine could have moved on of her own volition and none of this is what it seems."

"If the records hadn't been deleted I might agree with you," Catherine declared. "But they were, very thoroughly and deliberately – whoever did that had a damn good reason for doing so."

"I tend to agree," Frank nodded. "But Logan could still be right – we don't have a body that we know of, Christine may have been abducted and be being held somewhere. We need to keep an open mind on this."

"So, will the police department pick this up officially," Emma asked, looking at Sloane.

He looked at Frank and just said, "It feels bad."

"Hmm, I agree." Frank moved to the whiteboards and studied the information. "We only have a description of Christine...all her possessions were disposed of by the local council – which mean any photographs are gone."

Frank continued to muse and think out loud until Catherine took up his line of thinking.

"We need to get the Salvation Army Major together with an identification artist," she suggested. "And we need to open up the investigation."

"What are you thinking?" Logan asked, knowing that determined look on his wife's face.

"I'm thinking that Christine may not be the only victim," Catherine turned to Logan and saw that he'd already considered that possibility and smiled. "But you've already thought of that…good."

"If that's true, we're going to have a hard time tracing them," Emma put in. "It's not like we can look for similar cases or MO's – if he is killing them they're going to turn up as Jane Doe's and then they'll disappear entirely."

Sloane's frown deepened. "What do you mean by that – I don't get it?"

"I mean – it seems to me this man wants to wipe them out completely, wouldn't someone like that want to erase everything?" When Sloane only continued to frown, Emma rolled her eyes and continued her explanation, but not before she caught Catherine's smile of understanding. "If Jane Doe was found there would be a record somewhere, maybe even an autopsy as she'd be an unattended death at the very least. Our man doesn't like records, he deletes them completely. I'd say he'll follow up once he knows the Jane Doe has been found and will go back into the records to delete them also. She never existed," Emma finished ominously.

"He'd have to be careful on his timing," Catherine stated, looking at Emma as they worked through the problem.

"Yes. Yes he would," Emma agreed, catching on to Catherine's train of thought. "He'd only throw up suspicion if he deleted the records before she was buried – the morgue would be left with a body in their freezers that wouldn't automatically get referred to the local council for burial. Do that a few times and it would eventually get noticed by someone."

"I think our man's savvier than that," Catherine nodded. "He'll have plotted out a typical data trail that most of us have and the timing needed to erase it."

"Plus, we don't know how long he's been at this," Logan interjected. "He could be an old hand at this – maybe he even does it for a living in some industrial context?"

"An IT man, you mean?" Catherine nodded.

"If you're as good as he is with a computer wouldn't it make sense to earn a decent living from the skill?"

Catherine crossed to an unused whiteboard and began writing ideas on it, just words like 'IT man' and 'self-employed'.

"If he's doing what you think he is – all the stalking and background research – he'd need flexible hours to be able to carry it out," Sloane observed as he watched Catherine work. "I think the self-employed idea is a good one – he wouldn't have to answer to anyone, wouldn't have to account for his time in any way that matters."

When they were about to finish up, Catherine crossed to Frank and managed to guide him to one side.

"That Pathologist, Carl Haynes, that you often talk about, do you think he'd speak to me? Directly I mean," she added when Frank raised a quizzical brow.

"I'm sure I could arrange it. But why – the morgue is hardly pleasant and I couldn't guarantee that you wouldn't have to talk to him while he's working," Frank grimaced.

"I could be wrong, but I don't think watching an autopsy would be as distressing to me as you seem to think," Catherine tried to reassure Frank. "In fact, I think it would be fascinating to see the process that I've read so much about."

Frank looked at Catherine like he was trying to weigh her up, decide if she was in her right mind, and she laughed.

"I'm not a ghoul, but I am fascinated by the process, the information that can be gleaned from it," Catherine explained. "And I'd love to talk to someone who can give me some real insight."

Her eyes were intent on Frank's, her thirst for knowledge positively radiating off her.

"I'll arrange it," Frank said, and then he and Sloane left to go back to the station and write up what they'd learned and initiate some digging of their own.

"You actually want to watch an autopsy?" Emma grimaced as she crossed the room to make coffee.

"Yes. I know what they do and how they do it, but I've never seen it with my own eyes – unless you count video footage," Catherine added with a derisive chuckle that said she didn't.

"Why?" Emma asked, handing Logan and Catherine a steaming mug of coffee each. "Why do you even know that stuff – it's hardly bedtime reading?"

Now it was Logan's turn to chuckle and Emma turned to look at him. "You wouldn't want to know what Catherine's idea of bedtime reading includes. But autopsies and the work of a Pathologist are pleasant topics compared to other's my wife studies."

Turning to Catherine, Emma had just one word for what she thought about her reading habits. "Yuk!"

CHAPTER TEN

He took her into a secluded woods over 20 miles away. The shadow moved without making a sound, carrying the druggie over his shoulder with ease.

She fell to the ground with a heavy thunk when he yanked on her ankles. She was less than raw meat to him, less than the vermin that no doubt lived among the trees where he would leave her.

But before he did so, all identifying markers would be stripped from her including her clothes.

He went through the ritual with methodical efficiency, stripping her of clothing, cutting her hair, removing the pads of her fingers and toes and searching the body for any other possible tells.

She had one that was hidden on her inner thigh, a pink birthmark that was shaped like Australia.

He lit the end of a small branch, waited for it to get

really hot then extinguished the flame. As he had many times before, he pushed the smouldering end into the area of flesh with the birthmark and obliterated it.

"You'll make good food for the rats," he told the lifeless body of the druggie. "That's all you've ever been good for."

He took up a much larger branch, swinging it high over his head, and brought it down repeatedly on her head until her face was also obliterated.

"You're nothing! Nothing!" he groaned with every swing of the branch.

He stopped only when his arms ached from the effort, his face and body covered in her blood.

He'd never got this carried away before, but she'd made him angrier than the ones before her. She'd had a good home and tossed it off – she'd made her choices and now he'd finished her!

"It's scum like you who took my Mary, but you won't take anyone ever again. I'll wipe you off the face of the earth. You don't deserve to walk the same ground as decent people."

When Catherine awoke she turned over to face Logan then her eyes popped open and she sprang out of bed. Racing to the bathroom she bent over the toilet and wretched for all she was worth.

Logan came to crouch beside her, stroking her hair as

Catherine vomited violently into the bowl.

"You didn't get any of this last time," he fretted over her. "I think we need to get you to a doctor or, better still, I'll call one to come out to see you while you go back to bed."

"It's morning sickness, Logan, nothing they can do about it," Catherine told him when she was finally able to lift her head out of the loo.

Taking her elbow, Logan helped her to stand and waited while Catherine rinsed her mouth.

"I wish it were," Logan sighed. "But you get sick at odd times during the day, even during the night sometimes."

She turned to look at him, lifting a brow. "Adrianne had it really bad, much worse than me."

"But you didn't have it at all with the boys," he pointed out firmly.

"True, but from what Linda has told me, each pregnancy is different. Even the birth can be very different...apparently," she added with a grimace, not liking to think about that event.

They moved back into the bedroom and Catherine sat on the end of the bed.

"I don't think a visit to the morgue today is a very good idea," Logan began, pacing the bedroom in front of Catherine. "You don't want to throw up in front of Mr Haynes – I'm sure you'd find that possibility mortifying."

"If I thought that might happen I wouldn't be going," Catherine said, with an emphasis on the words that said she had every intention of going as planned.

When he stopped pacing and just looked down at her, Catherine shrugged and said, "I won't get sick because of the autopsy – it doesn't work like that."

"How do you know?" he asked impatiently. "You've never had morning sickness before and you've sure as hell never witnessed a live autopsy before!"

"And we don't know that I will today – though Carl seemed amenable to the idea," Catherine mused.

"Carl? He's Carl now?!" Logan wasn't just frowning, now his eyes were boring into her.

"We talked on the phone for ages," Catherine shrugged. "You can't discuss body parts and forensic testing of bodily fluids and not end up on first name terms. You just can't," she told him.

By the time Catherine left for the morgue she was feeling much steadier and had even managed to keep down a small breakfast.

She actually felt buzzed at the prospect of meeting Carl Haynes in the flesh. She'd really enjoyed their talk on the phone and was sure he'd be even more forthcoming when they talked face to face.

When they shook hands Catherine was surprised by the gentle touch of the man who carved up bodies for a living. His skin was soft and his fingers held hers with just enough force to give a little squeeze of welcome.

"I must admit, I wasn't sure you'd come," Carl Haynes grinned, his handsome face lighting up with amusement. "But I'm very glad you did."

"My husband wasn't sure that I should come," Catherine smiled, not sure why she felt the need to point out the fact that she was married.

"Why is that?" Carl asked as he showed her through to his office and offered Catherine a seat.

"I'm pregnant – I'm throwing up at the drop of a hat at the most inopportune times. But I can promise you that I don't feel nauseous at this precise moment and I usually get plenty of warning when I do," she assured him.

He was frowning over at her, assessing Catherine with concerned eyes. "I'll arrange for you to sit during the autopsy – and I suggest you sit in the auditorium rather than enter the lab itself."

"But I want to be able to ask questions, to see the finer details and get a feel for the process," she protested.

He liked her enthusiasm, enjoyed her quick mind and had been looking forward to her visit today, and Carl realised that he too was disappointed.

"I'm not sure – you would have to be absolutely positive that you wouldn't get ill anywhere near my patient," Carl said, knowing that he'd already accepted the idea of Catherine entering his lab.

"Not a problem – if I get the merest hint of nausea I'll be out of there in a blink," she assured him.

But she didn't get sick. Catherine was too intrigued to even think about getting sick.

"And here…" Catherine pointed to an area of the body where a gash rent the skin of the dead man's thigh, "…is this some kind of tool mark?"

Carl was grinning from ear to ear when he came to stand at Catherine's side to examine the wound she was pointing to. "It certainly is," Carl proclaimed, pleased that she'd spotted the tell-tale signs. "Do you have any idea what the tool might have been?"

She considered the markings, turned her head this way and that to assess them. "Actually, I think it's more likely to be the hilt of a knife – one thrust into the victim at an angle which is why the gash is longer than the blade would be wide. But this looks to be the hilt mark…" and she pointed to the left side of the gash, "…left when the attacker pushed it hard against the thigh leaving this odd shaped bruise, as well as these other markings."

"Very good," Carl congratulated her. "So, what about these injuries, do you think the same weapon was used?"

Catherine peered at the puncture wounds to the chest and abdomen and nodded. "The hilt marks look almost identical – I think the variation can be accounted for by the angle of insertion. I also think these wounds show a blade width of around 1" – I can't say about the length."

When the autopsy was over, Carl asked Catherine to wait for him in his office while he finished up.

She helped herself to a bottle of water from the little fridge, as Carl had invited her to, and sat looking around the tidy office and the shelves of books – some of which she had read.

"How are you feeling?" Carl asked when he strode into his office and sat behind the large oak desk.

"I'm fine, though the water was very welcome, thank you," Catherine smiled, holding the bottle up.

"And your feet – a lot of people find it difficult to stand for so long when they're not used to it," Carl clarified when her brow went up.

"Oh, I see. Well, I deliberately wore flats for comfort and these are some of the oldest shoes I own," she grinned.

Returning her grin, Carl nodded enthusiastically. "Don't you just have to keep them – I have a pair that must be going on 7 years old. I keep getting them re-soled and heeled and even re-stitched rather than throw them away. Comfort is everything," he chuckled at himself.

"Are you married?" Catherine asked out of the blue.

Carl's head tipped to one side as he considered the question. "No, I'm not – why do you ask?"

"It's just, since I married Logan, and even before if truth be told, he's been chucking out my old sweats and replacing them with expensive dresses or linen trousers," Catherine snorted in disgust. "It just crossed my mind that if you had a wife you probably wouldn't still have the 7 year old shoes."

When Carl erupted with laughter, Catherine found herself joining him.

"That's some observation, and probably true," Carl told her when his laughter died. "Now, I know you wanted to talk to me as well as watch an actual post-mortem exam – which you handled brilliantly," he smiled with a nod of his head. "So how can I help you?"

Her smile died and Catherine pulled all the information they'd gathered on the Christine Wakelin case to the front of her mind.

After outlining what they already knew, Catherine told him of their speculations.

"If we're right and he is using his tech skills to clear the way for murder, then he's probably done it before," Catherine said, screwing the cap back on the bottle of water after taking a sip.

"What makes you think that?"

"It's too good – I doubt he was as thorough with his first attempt at wiping someone's complete life data," she speculated. "Although he left a few breadcrumbs in the works, his tech skills are excellent – anyone else might not have found them."

Carl's brows winged up at her unabashed immodesty. "You consider yourself the best at what you do?" he asked, already knowing the answer.

"I don't believe in false modesty," Catherine proclaimed without embarrassment. "I have an extremely high IQ and a near photographic memory…and I work at being at the top of my game…whatever that game may be."

Sitting back in his seat, Carl regarded Catherine with open admiration. "I like that, you know who you are and go with it. But what can I do to help you find Christine's abductor, possible murderer?"

Sitting forward in her seat, Catherine clasped her hands together on her knees and got down to business.

"You must get a fair number of John and Jane Doe's through your doors – I'm interested in the ones that show signs of having their identifiers removed or destroyed in some way. Maybe their fingertips were burned, tattoos removed or disfigured to make them untraceable?"

Shifting in his seat, Carl looked more than a little uncomfortable. "I wouldn't normally talk to anyone other than the police about such matters." He hesitated, regarding Catherine with eyes that seemed to see right into her soul. "But…Frank wouldn't have suggested I talk to you if he didn't completely trust you so I need to be able to do the same," Carl told her, towering his fingers so that the tips touched then raised them to his lips. "Any information we discuss has to stay between us, is that clear?"

But Catherine surprised him by shaking her head. "I won't lie to you – I have a partner...two partners actually," she corrected, remembering that Logan was a partner now too. "I need to be able to discuss anything you tell me with them, but I can promise that no information will leave our office – is that good enough?"

Carl rubbed the back of his neck and sighed. "That's a lot more people to trust than I'm comfortable with but, again, Frank obviously knows your set up and he has told me that he sometimes works with you. So...alright...I'm going to trust you to keep your word."

CHAPTER ELEVEN

On the drive back to the office, Catherine found herself wondering about the information Carl had divulged. Once he'd decided to trust her and her partners, he'd been very forthcoming about some events that were possibly connected to Emma's case.

He'd had a couple of Jane and John Doe's months apart, but now he thought about it there were similarities between them.

The John Doe, the first to arrive on his table, had had all of his fingertips burned almost through to the bone. Carl had told the detective on the case about the odd injuries but they hadn't been able to close the case – it had been assumed that he was an indigent who'd been tortured.

Apparently that happened a lot to the homeless – they get treated as non-humans, just so much litter cluttering up the streets and parks.

But when Carl had tried to find the case on his computer he hadn't been able to.

"That ties in with our thoughts on how this would play out," Catherine had told him. "We had speculated that he would wait until the body had been referred to the local authorities for burial and then he'd wipe the records clean. No more John Doe, no similar crimes for the police to track and start looking at more closely."

Carl had been understandably angry when he realised that his records had been tampered with and said he would be discussing their security with the powers-that-be in management.

When he found no trace of the more recent Jane Doe, whose fingertips had been removed with a sharp implement, Carl Haynes became incensed, he'd also got on the phone to Frank and reported the situation formally.

Before she left, Catherine told him about CompuSafe, the company she used to own that wrote and installed comprehensive security software. "Ben Sharman owns it now – I wanted to branch out in a different direction, but he's also really good. And he's using a couple of programmes that I wrote myself so I can recommend those too."

She hadn't seen Ben in a while, at least not to say

anything other than 'hi' to as they'd passed each other in the street.

He'd thought himself in love with her once, and Catherine had called herself all kinds of a fool for not realising sooner.

But I do miss you, Ben. We could always talk and had a few good laughs…I had no idea that I was hurting you.

And that was why she'd tried to avoid him since. She didn't want to be responsible for raking up old hurts and hoped he'd moved on with his life

Still, if Carl wants to upgrade his computer security I couldn't recommend anyone better. I hope Ben gets the job.

When Catherine got home she went straight to the kitchen breakfast room to see her boys. Henry and Linda seemed to spend most of their time in this comfortable room and so the boys did too.

It was a miserable day, cold and windy with a sky full of rain clouds, definitely not a day for taking the twins outdoors. When she walked into the carpeted breakfast area she found the boys laying on a blanket practicing rolling over.

"Look at my clever boys," Catherine crooned as she took her coat off and moved to kneel next to them. Bending forward she nuzzled her face between them and, as they often did, the boys patted her cheeks with their little hands.

"Is Logan back," she asked Henry who was sitting on a small settee along the back wall of the large breakfast area, and just behind where the boys were playing.

"Not yet," Henry frowned. "He phoned half an hour ago, said he was in a meeting with the prospective buyer for the estate agency. Didn't sound like he'd be home any time soon."

She grimaced, not only because she didn't envy him the stressful task of selling a multi-million pound company, but also because he was letting go of something he and his father had built up over many years.

He'd already spoken to her about how long it had taken him to come to terms with his decision. Not that Logan regretted the decision he had finally come to – his family would always come before money. But he did feel guilty that he wouldn't be passing on the company to his sons as his father had proudly passed it on to him.

"He's suffering guilt pangs," Catherine smiled up at Henry. "You built that company, passed it on to Logan and he feels that perhaps he should be hanging on to it to pass on to our sons."

"But that isn't what Logan truly wants," Henry told her. "And, because I know that, it isn't what I want either. My son's happiness is my only concern. I just wish he could get it over with so that you can all move on," he sighed.

"Thanks, Henry. I know that means a lot to Logan, as it does to me," Catherine smiled.

"So, how did your meeting with the Pathologist go – get any more leads?" Henry asked with a comic jiggle of his eyebrows.

She grimaced again and nodded. "Unfortunately It looks like we were right, there does appear to be more victims and they've ended up at the morgue. So…" she sighed, sitting back on her heels, "…it doesn't look hopeful that our missing person will be found alive."

"Well now, you just keep your hopes up and you never know what miracles might happen," Henry smiled. "We have two little miracles right here, and a third on the way – maybe even a fourth," he grinned impishly.

"I know when you're stirring things up," she wagged a finger at Henry. "Logan's been talking to you, hasn't he?"

"Guilty," Henry chuckled, then his face became serious and his eyes filled with concern. "You and the boys are his world now – he's worried about you, and he has a lot of worry on his plate already just now."

His shot hit home, probably harder and more deeply than Henry intended, but Catherine was spurred into action and filled with remorse.

"Hell's teeth, I am such a selfish so-and-so!" Looking down at Andrew and Adam, her guilt only deepened. Both were so like their daddy and both were smiling up at her with contented innocence in their beautiful eyes.

She gave them both a hug, breathing in their unique scent to take a part of them with her. "I need to go up to the office," she told Henry, just as Linda came in from the utility room out back.

When she saw Catherine's troubled expression the smile she'd been wearing in greeting slipped. "Has something happened?"

"No, just me being my usual selfish self," Catherine told her. Then she left to go to the office and let Henry fill Linda in on the details.

She took the stairs two at a time, swung the office door open and let it thud closed as she strode over to her desk. Emma raised a brow but didn't speak – she knew better than to invite Catherine to chew her head off.

She heard Catherine on the telephone arranging an appointment for a scan with her Obstetrician. Then she watched as her friend held her head in her hands and looked miserable.

"Ok, I might be taking my life in my hands but I can't sit here and watch you suffer – what the hell happened, did the Pathologist turn up something really awful?" Emma asked. "Or is this about the baby – I couldn't help overhearing your phone conversation?"

Closing her eyes, Catherine took a deep breath and let it out slowly. "It's about me – about the terrible person

I've always been and always will be."

Her misery was so deep, some wound laid open that Emma could only guess had to do with her childhood. She didn't know everything about Catherine, but Emma knew enough to know that the hurt was real and never really went away.

"Catherine, I can attest that you have a temper, that you don't always use a lot of tact when you have something to say. But you are not a bad person," Emma insisted quietly. "You'd give your life to save any member of your family – you almost did not so long ago," she reminded Catherine.

She had watched Catherine fall into a coma in this very room after working some psychic miracle to help save her sister, Caroline.

That day would stay with Emma for ever, she was sure. Logan had torn into Neil Farraday as though he would kill him when the psychic who had been working with Catherine couldn't wake her up.

"That's different," Catherine stated, not raising her eyes from her desk. "It wasn't a choice, I did what I had to do, nothing more."

Deciding that sympathy wasn't helping, Emma braced herself for a verbal slugging match. "Ok, you want to indulge in a pity party I won't stop you. Just don't expect me to join in."

Just as she'd hoped, Catherine's head flew up and her eyes were blazing. "Pity party! I do not do pity parties!"

"Oh yes you do," Emma insisted. "That's exactly what this is – you've done or not done something or other and now you're taking on all the blame. Well I've got news for you…" Emma stood, hands on hips facing Catherine, "…we are all capable of being selfish, unthinking, bull-headed and inconsiderate – that just makes us human, not bad people!"

Stumped, Catherine found herself at a loss for words. If she wasn't careful it might become a habit.

"Well hell!" Catherine sat back in her seat and frowned up at Emma. "I thought we were going to go a few rounds – then you had to come up with all that reasonable stuff and ruined it!"

Laughing, Emma crossed the room and got two mugs out to make them some coffee. "I did, didn't I?"

"No need to look so smug about it – I was in just the right mood for a good fight," Catherine complained.

All laughter gone, Emma came to sit on the corner of Catherine's desk and simply asked, "Why?"

Grimacing at her own thoughts, Catherine finally confessed. "I thought I was getting better at this family stuff – you know, all the 'there there's' and 'how are you' type things."

Emma struggled not to laugh at the image Catherine

put in her head, but her pained expression kept her quiet.

"But when it comes to the important stuff, I'm just as useless as I always was," Catherine sighed.

"You know, you're going to have to spell it out…" Emma said dryly, "…I don't have your psychic abilities."

That made Catherine grimace and Emma laughed as she got up to finish making the coffee.

"Do you have to remind me?!"

Her 'psychic ability', as Emma put it, was something Catherine chose to ignore when she could. Though thinking about it right now, she had to wonder why it hadn't raised its weird and scary head lately.

Maybe I'm losing it? Hey, maybe it's gone and I'll be completely normal from now on – or as normal as I can be given my lack of social skills.

"You're smiling…" Emma noted when she returned with their coffees, "…did you get one of your 'visions'?"

Picking up her coffee, Catherine leaned back in her seat and looked at Emma with a curious frown. "As a matter of fact…no," she laughed when Emma went wide eyed, "…I was just thinking that I hadn't had anything like that in a while. Do you think it's gone?"

"Do you?" Emma asked in turn.

"How the heck do I know – I don't really know anything about that stuff?!"

"Which is weird when you think about it," Emma told

her. "I mean, you know a lot about a lot of things – you read the most obscure and, honestly, boring books you can get your hands on and remember just about everything in them. Yet you've never read up on your psychic ability – why?" she asked, dumbfounded.

"I wish you wouldn't keep calling it that," Catherine grimaced over her coffee.

"What should I call it – the All Seeing Eye, or your own personal mind control? You know, like when you made yourself visible to Wade and made her believe that you were Caroline's ghost," Emma chuckled.

"Jesus, will you just stop – you're freaking me out?!" and Catherine shuddered uncomfortably. "I don't have an All Seeing Eye, and I especially don't have any kind of mind control. What the hell kind of TV have you been watching?"

Laughing at Catherine's disgusted expression, Emma took her mug of coffee back to her desk and sat down.

She was well aware that Catherine had avoided telling her what specifically had upset her, but Emma was good with that. Her friend looked a lot happier than she had and that had been her goal.

CHAPTER TWELVE

Once she'd mulled things over and written up an account of her meeting with the Pathologist, Catherine felt much better. She still believed she was a moron where relationships were concerned, but Logan had known that before he'd married her, and he still had so he must not mind her lack of ability in that department. Or, she hoped he didn't.

"I need to fill you in on what I learned from the Pathologist," she told Emma, waiting for her colleague to finish what she was doing. "I told him our theory, that this man could be deleting the data footprints of his victims with a view to carrying out the perfect murder – an untraceable murder," Catherine added.

"And did he agree?" Emma asked, sitting back in her seat and looking at Catherine with eager interest.

"He did – especially when he thought of the two

bodies that he hadn't been able to identify – they'd had their fingerprints eradicated," Catherine informed her.

Emma's brows shot up and she sat forward to ask, "How – did he burn them or use some form of acid?"

"Yuk!" Catherine grimaced, though Emma hadn't been far off the mark. "No to the acid but yes to the burning with the first victim. The second one had the pads of their fingers sliced off – hopefully after they were dead but I forgot to ask about that."

Now it was Emma's turn to say, "Yuk! So how come Frank and Sloane didn't mention these two victims – it seems to me they could be related, don't you think?"

"I do. But Frank and Sloane were not the investigating officers, there was no reason for them to know about them," Catherine pointed out. "The victims were not related at the time – apart from the fingerprints being eradicated, the second victim had very different injuries, and not all of those were post-mortem."

"What kind of injuries," Emma asked, somewhat reluctantly.

"She had her face bashed in so bad that identification, even by dental records, would have been impossible," Catherine recalled matter of fact.

"Maybe that was the perp's form of escalation," Emma speculated. "And we don't know that she was his next victim, only that she was the second noticed at that particular morgue – what if he's moving around or dispersing the bodies so as not to raise suspicion?"

"Hmm, could be he got lucky with these two - they were investigated separately and by different detectives so no connection was ever made."

"But surely they would have shown up as like crimes," Emma said, then rolled her eyes in exasperation. "Their records were wiped, weren't they?"

"They were," Catherine nodded. "And our friendly Pathologist was none too pleased when he realised that someone had hacked into his system to wipe them. I haven't spoken to Frank yet, but I bet he'll find they've been wiped off the police records as well."

"So...how do we trace them? No doubt the council will have buried them and their records will have been wiped too – this is too scary to be real," Emma declared ominously. "This maniac may actually have pulled off the perfect murder – though I won't mention that to Sloane."

Catherine got up to pace the room, pulling many lines of thought together. "I know we're no longer just up the road but, do you think Sloane and Frank would be amenable to another meeting – I really think we should discuss this with them face to face?"

"I'll give Sloane a call," Emma offered. "I don't think they'll object considering what we've uncovered."

Although her mind was partially distracted by her

continued efforts to track the hacker back to his computer, Catherine still had time to think about Logan.

She had thought he would be back by now but was sure he would have come up to the office if he was home.

If only she could do something – Catherine hated feeling helpless. Logan was always taking care of her, the one time he was struggling with something and there was absolutely nothing she could do to help him.

Maybe she could take his mind off his troubles for a bit – but how?

He knows I don't cook and I wouldn't have a clue what to buy him as a surprise. How come he's so good at this stuff and I suck at it?!

Suddenly Catherine's mind was a million miles away from Logan as she made the breakthrough she'd been working towards. "I've got him – I'm in!" she said, just as Sloane and Frank, followed by Logan, entered the office.

"In where?" Logan asked with some concern. He knew the kinds of places Catherine and Emma were likely to hack into and didn't like the look of glee on his wife's face.

"I'm in the perp's computer," she said, shaking her head in wonder. "Now I can start looking through his files and see what information I can find on his victims."

Everyone was staring at her as Catherine started tapping keys in rapid fire succession. "No. No. No. No. He's wiped his files – I'm picking up bits and pieces but most of its gone. Shit!"

She was so frustrated Catherine didn't even notice that she had sworn.

"You didn't get anything…?" Sloane asked, his voice incredulous and angry at the same time.

It earned him a scowl from Logan that stopped him in his tracks when he would have marched over to Catherine's desk.

Stepping in quickly, Frank moved forward and said, "Are you able to pin down a location – perhaps if we got our hands on the actual computer you could dig out more information?"

"Yes," Catherine nodded, her fingers going back to work. It took a few minutes but then Catherine said, "Upper Stanton – 103 Station Road!"

When she made to stand and go with Sloane and Frank, Logan stepped into her path, effectively blocking it.

"You don't need to be there for the retrieval – let the police handle it," he told her when Catherine made to push past him.

"But I'm the one who found him, and it's our case!" she protested when he didn't move.

"It's a police matter now," Sloane told her. "Though I know you'll continue to work the missing persons' angle, we'll be taking any murder cases arising."

"Oh really!" Catherine stood, hands on hips, her eyes

blazing. "And who do you think will be able to get all the information off the computer you're going to collect — because if you're not very careful you'll probably trigger a failsafe that will trash the hard-drive?!"

"We do have computer experts on the force," Sloane said disparagingly. "Not that we aren't grateful for your assistance, but this is a police matter now."

She looked at Frank and saw he was hesitating so pushed her luck. "Frank? Are you really going to take this out of our hands?"

He looked uncomfortable, hesitated, then seemed to get an idea that made him smile. "No, I'm not, but whether you continue to work on this case is entirely up to you," he said cryptically.

"If it's up to me then I say yes," Catherine told him, and gave Sloane a look of triumph.

"Good — then you won't mind coming into the station to sign a Consultancy Contract," Frank smiled.

Catherine frowned, not entirely sure what she was getting herself and her company into. "Exactly how does that work — I'd still be working for myself, right?"

"No, you'd be working for the Sheriton Police Department as a Consultant for the duration of the case," Frank told her, his voice firm. "That means taking orders and following them to the letter. Your specialist consultancy area would, of course, be computers and all matters concerning them. But you would have to stick within the law when working on anything directly connected to a case – is that clear?"

She looked to Logan and then Emma, when they both nodded their agreement Catherine gave Frank his answer.

"Ok then, you've got yourself a computer consultant," she smiled. "So do I get to examine the perp's computer?"

He nodded, but Frank said, "We are going to retrieve the computer from the address you gave us while you go into the station and request to fill out a consultancy contract – I'll contact them so that they'll be expecting you and have one ready for you to sign. Ok?"

She grimaced, but Catherine knew when she was outmanoeuvred. "I'll get it done, just make sure no one tampers with that computer before I take a look at it."

When Frank and Sloane had gone, Catherine turned to Logan and Emma with a confused look on her face.

"How the hell did I go from working for our company to working for the police…?" she asked them, lifting her hands then letting them fall to her sides.

With a deep chuckle, Logan pushed off the desk he was leaning against and walked over to her. "My wife the cop – whatever next?"

She punched his arm, wincing at the thought. "I am not a cop, I'm a Computer Consultant. And even that is only while I'm working on a case with Frank."

With a cheeky smile Emma said, "You do realise that Sloane will also be your boss – if he tells you to jump you have to ask how high and say, yes sir."

For just a blink of time Catherine looked stunned, and then she looked stubborn and determined. "Not on your life! I'll take orders from Frank but Shivers had better stay out of my way. He'd just love to tell me what to do, but he can dream on!"

Both Logan and Emma laughed at her outrage.

"Don't wind him up and you should get along just fine," Emma cautioned Catherine. "He has great respect for what you do – he just doesn't like the way you go about doing it," she added when Catherine raised a disbelieving brow.

Deciding not to remind Emma that she went about things in the exact same way, Catherine just shook it off.

"We have an appointment with the Obstetrician tomorrow at 2:30," Catherine told Logan, and watched the significance dawn on him. She shrugged, "It was time."

When he took her in his arms and hugged her, Catherine snuggled into him. "I'm sorry, I'm such an idiot when it comes to this stuff." Tipping her face up to look at him, she said, "I didn't mean to worry you, sorry."

Giving her an adoring smile, Logan kissed her so thoroughly that all thought of Emma went out of her mind. She kissed him back eagerly, glad that she hadn't screwed things up any worse than she had – from now on she would make herself stop and think how her actions affected others – how they affected Logan.

When he lifted his lips from hers and the world stopped spinning, Catherine finally thought of Emma and quickly looked around the office for her.

"She's gone home," Logan told her with a wicked smile. "Emma's got an excellent sense of when 3 is just 1 too many people in a room. I must remember to thank her."

Relaxing back into his wonderfully strong arms, Catherine allowed a deep sigh to escape her and he pulled her in closer.

"I love you for who you are, Catherine – nothing will ever change that," he told her, sensing her insecurity.

She could feel his large, comforting hands stroking up and down her back and wanted them on her in a much more intimate way. When she lifted her face to his and pulled his mouth down to hers, Catherine left him in no doubt as to what she wanted and when.

Her body thrummed as they fit snuggly together, his hardness pressing into her, gloriously ready to meet her needs. And she would give him all of herself, heart and soul, everything that she was in every way that he wanted, just as long as he kept wanting her.

"I love you, Logan."

"I love you, too – every second of every day – my darling wife."

He carried her out of the office and into their bedroom, snicking the lock just in case.

As he lay her gently on the bed, Catherine felt all the worries and misgivings leave her, just lift away to be replaced by a myriad of very different emotions.

She watched him strip off his shirt, his eyes never leaving hers. His chest was an impressive wall of muscle that he honed in the gym each day and used on the rugby pitch to intimidate the opposition.

He was like a ferocious warrior when he played rugby, but here, in the bedroom, he was her gentle giant, so loving, so giving, so...

"Oh god," she moaned as his hands slid up her legs and his thumbs began to work their magic between her thighs.

She was instantly wet for him, her body responding to his touch as if made especially for him. Catherine forgot about going to the police station – hell, she couldn't have told anyone her own name, such was Logan's ability to take her over, body and mind.

Without knowing when it happened, Catherine found herself naked under him until Logan rolled to pull her atop him.

"Just look at you…" he crooned, his dark brown voice soft and sexy, his eyes molten with love and lust, "…all woman and sexy as hell."

His hands cupped her full breasts and kneaded them, his thumbs flicking over the hard nipples in a way that made her grind her crotch into him.

She lifted herself and guided him in. All of him…the full hard length of him slid home and filled her with pleasure.

His groan, so guttural and sexy, only spurred her on. She wanted to hear it again, and again, and her hips pistoned until they were both groaning in unison.

They communicated so well in the bedroom, no words were needed to say I love you. They touched, explored, drove each other wild, and when the storm hit they would ride it together – at that moment they were one…they always would be.

<u>CHAPTER THIRTEEN</u>

Getting out of Logan's Range Rover, Catherine felt her cheeks heat at the thought of what had made her late.

How could she have forgotten the damned consultant contract? And what if Sloane and Frank arrived back at the office before she and Logan got home – they'd know something had delayed her and, with the tell-tale signs of her embarrassment, it wouldn't take much to guess what it had been. *Oh christ, let's just get this done and get back home!*

As it happened, no one was as put out as Catherine herself. The officer manning the desk produced the necessary document and handed it over, indicating a room she might like to use to fill it in and handing her a pen.

"Do you think this is one of those interrogation rooms?" she asked Logan when they sat at the desk.

He grinned and asked, "Why are you whispering, they're not going to grill you. Or have you done something you haven't told me about?"

She frowned at him, then smiled at his boyish grin. He really twisted her heart at the most unexpected moments, she realised.

"No, I haven't – have you?"

But Catherine lowered her gaze to the contract in front of her and began filling it in.

"Hell, they want to know some pretty personal stuff," she complained, but signed it anyway.

"I suppose they have to ask those kinds of things to be able to check that you're a stand-up citizen," Logan told her. "They can't just take your word for it, or Frank's either."

"I suppose not."

The desk officer took the completed form and said, "Welcome on board, hope to see you soon."

Just that simple greeting placated Catherine somewhat. It was nice to think that not all people expected the worst in people – he'd assumed she was a stand-up citizen until proved otherwise. *Nice one!*

She was relieved to find that they had, indeed, beat Sloane and Frank back to the house. Henry and Linda were getting ready to sit down to dinner and the boys were in their bouncy chairs, happily watching the grown-ups.

Their smiles were instant, both boys kicking their legs and flailing their arms when Catherine and Logan entered the room.

They instinctively took turns for which boy they picked up – this time Logan got Andrew and Catherine got Adam.

"Mmm," they said in unison as they hugged the child they were holding and breathed them in.

"How did it go today – didn't get a chance to talk to you when you got home?" Henry asked Logan.

Catherine closed her eyes, despairing that she would ever learn to deal with the relationship stuff – she hadn't even thought to ask him about his meeting.

Seeing her distress, Logan slipped his free arm round her waist and pulled his family close. "We signed the papers today – Mac Hargreaves was just trying to wangle a few extras without paying for them – computer systems and the like," he expounded when his father frowned.

"You've not long had it all upgraded – some people want something for nothing no matter how sweet the deal is in the first place," Henry shook his head in disgust. "Now, come and get some dinner – Linda has cooked us a mean chilli-con-carne," he grinned.

Catherine was about to explain about Frank and Sloane being due back when her mobile rang.

"Sorry…" she said, handing Adam to his grandad, "…I need to take this."

When she came back into the room, Logan could see that all had not gone well.

"The house was empty – they'd missed him by about an hour – Frank was really p…" She caught herself and stumbled over her words.

"I get the drift," Logan frowned. "So, after all that there's no computer to analyse."

"No," Catherine confirmed, her lips pursed. "They could see where he'd been working and it was cleared out."

"And Christine?"

Shaking her head, she said, "No sign of her having been there – but apparently the place was a tip, so who knows."

"Well, let's enjoy a nice meal together," Linda invited, taking Adam from Henry and settling him in his bouncy chair as Logan did the same with Andrew. "I've made a nice apple crumble with custard for afters," she smiled at Catherine, knowing the younger woman had a sweet tooth.

"Oh wow, now my stomach is growling," Catherine said, rubbing it hungrily.

She'd missed lunch, it hadn't entered her head, but she didn't want Logan to know about that. Things had just happened and time had gotten away from her. But she was ready for the mouth-watering meal that Linda was busy dishing up.

This had been the first day that Catherine hadn't suffered with sickness. She hoped she was getting past it as Linda had told her she might.

"We have an appointment at the hospital tomorrow," Logan said as Linda handed him a very full plate. "Will you be alright to have the boys?"

He knew his dad and Linda loved having them, but he didn't want to take it for granted. After all, it wouldn't be any trouble to take the twins with them if they had other plans.

"Not a problem," Henry assured him. "The weatherman said it'll be mild tomorrow – might take them out to the lake to feed the ducks."

It was so nice to sit and eat a meal with family – her family, Catherine reminded herself yet again. The miracle of what Logan had brought her still had the power to bring her to tears at the oddest moments. Thankfully, the tears were being put down to her pregnancy and Catherine said nothing to disabuse them.

But tonight was different, Catherine felt all warm and fuzzy inside, especially when the topic turned to Christmas.

"Dad and I thought it would be nice to open up the old ballroom," Logan explained. "It needs a lot of work so we'll have to get started on it asap."

"What kind of work – not more construction?" she grimaced at the memory of all the work that had gone into making Lakelands their ideal home.

"No, no, nothing as major as that," Henry put in. "But it will want the old panelling ripping out and a lot of redecorating – we thought Caroline might be open to overseeing it all, seeing as she did such a good job on your rooms," Henry said, raising an inquisitive brow.

"I bet she'd love it," Catherine chuckled, knowing how much her sister loved shopping. How she ever managed to coordinate things the way she did was a mystery to Catherine, and one she was quite happy not to solve, thank you very much. "I bet she'd sort out the playground at the same time."

But Logan shook his head. "No, that's ok, I've already started on that."

That surprised Catherine, he hadn't said anything to her about it since they'd discussed it with Henry by the lake.

"Oh, ok," she nodded, secretly pleased that Logan was taking such a personal interest. After all, it was for their children and no one would be more mindful of their safety than a parent.

When Linda served up the apple crumble and put a jug of hot custard in the middle of the table, Catherine thought she had died and gone to heaven.

She could already smell the nutmeg that Linda used for flavouring, and the vanilla she added to the custard, which was totally home-made.

"Oh baby, you are in for a treat," Catherine stroked her stomach lovingly, making Logan laugh.

Pouring the creamy custard over the crumble, Catherine's eyes rounded in delight. But when she tasted the first spoonful of her favourite dessert she let out the kind of sigh that Logan had only ever heard her make in the bedroom.

"Now this is apple crumble as it was meant to be – mum always used nutmeg," Catherine said, closing her eyes to savour the flavour and the memory.

It was Logan's turn to feel his heart clench, to be glad that Catherine had allowed him to bring her these small pleasures by marrying him. He would buy her diamonds and silk if it would make her happy, but Logan knew that money and gifts meant little to Catherine, only that he had given them.

Even the engagement ring he'd had made for her had taken a lot of hard reasoning for him to get it on her finger. Catherine had protested at the large square cut diamond, the insane cost of it – though he'd kept the actual amount carefully hidden from her. If she'd known that her wild guesses were nowhere near the actual purchase price she would never have accepted it.

He loved giving her the best, spoiling her as she'd never been spoiled as a child. If he could give her anything, it would be love, and he made sure to do that every single day in as many ways as he could think of.

"You look lost in thought." Catherine leaned close to Logan to whisper to him.

When he smiled at her she saw his heart in his eyes and caught her breath. How the gods had blessed her.

CHAPTER FOURTEEN

"You're going too fast, Mr," Christine told the shadow as he moved through the night, his laptop under his arm.

"If you want to come with me you have to keep up," he told her, not unkindly. "Otherwise, I'll have to leave you behind." But what he didn't tell her was she would be dead, just like all the others, if he did.

He still didn't know why he'd kept her around, only she seemed more child than woman, and he didn't hold with killing kids. The ones who lived on the street didn't have a choice, but their parents were another matter. Sometimes, taking care of them set the child free and got them proper care.

Snuffing out the parents didn't cause him any second thoughts, they were scum of the earth and the world was better off without them!

Murdering bastards – thieving, murdering bastards!

They weren't going far – he'd already scouted out the next squat. It was an old bungalow, run down and overgrown it had been let go since the old lady who'd lived there had died.

He'd known her in better times – his Mary had run errands for her and done a little cleaning to keep the house as best she could. But Mary had been of poor health herself, she'd had early onset arthritis in all her joints, but she'd never let it get her down.

She worked through the pain, never took money from benefits and still managed to help others out. She was a jewel of a woman, a kind hearted soul who was taken in the cruellest way. But I'll make them pay, Mary. I'll make them pay for everything they did to you!

They were in luck, he wouldn't have to leech off the neighbours electricity supply. The old lady had only been dead this past fortnight, her relatives obviously hadn't gotten around to having the power supply turned off.

"No!" he spat out in hushed tones when Christine reached for a light switch. "We never put the lights on, I told you that before!"

"Sorry, Mr. I'm a good girl, my mummy always said I was a good girl," she pleaded, scared by his sudden anger.

"Just get inside," he told her, having used the key under the plant-pot to open the back door.

He didn't know how the police had found him, but

he'd managed to get out just in time and get the lump of a girl over the back fence before they'd realised what was happening.

But he'd have to go back for the van, it was parked down the road and there was no reason for them to know that it was his. So he would wait, give them time to do their nosing around and then he'd go back for it.

He'd planned to clean up another mess tonight, but now he would have to wait, his tools were in that van and he needed them to do his job properly.

If Catherine had only known that she had saved a life that night, she might have slept better. But worry about their hospital appointment the next day kept her awake.

What if I am having twins again – it isn't unheard of to have multiple sets of twins. I just don't know how we'll manage four babies under 1 year old – it doesn't bear thinking about.

But Catherine couldn't turn her thoughts off. The whys and wherefores of the situation just kept rolling around her head until she fell into an uncomfortable sleep.

At first it was more of the same, a continuation of the worries and practicalities of looking after 4 babies. But then the dream changed, morphed into a Christmas scene that must have been at least three years on.

Andrew and Adam were little men, helping a toddler

to open her presents. She was blond, blue eyed and the image of Catherine, and she could manage opening her own presents, thank you very much.

She must have been around 2, and she already had a mind of her own. Then the strangest thing happened – the little girl turned and smiled at Catherine as though she could see her, not just in the dream but for real.

Still in sleep, Catherine didn't feel the warm tears that slipped from her eyes and down the side of her face. She was smiling into the darkness, but her heart was filled with the light of a mother's love.

"Hey, Katy, that one's mine," Andrew told his little sister who seemed to think anything wrapped was hers to open. "Here, you can open that one – it's from Grandma," he smiled.

And there was Linda, surrounded by the children with Henry at her side. There was something different about them, but Catherine couldn't put her finger on it. She only felt that something had changed between them.

When Logan looked at her, Catherine felt her heart lurch – he too seemed to see her as clearly as Katy had.

Somehow Catherine knew this wasn't a dream – this was happening and she was a part of it. Her 'gift' was back and was showing her a scene from Christmas future.

He was leaning up on his elbow when Catherine awoke and opened her eyes to see Logan's handsome face staring down at her.

"I've been watching you for the last 10 minutes," he told her, his smile lighting up his lovely brown eyes. "I don't think I've ever seen you look as beautiful as you did just then – you were smiling and, even with your eyes closed, you looked so happy."

She was still smiling, though a little shyly. It was embarrassing to think he'd been watching her that way.

"As it happens I still feel happy – I have a feeling everything is going to be ok at the hospital today," she told him, reaching up to touch his face.

He covered her hand with his own and asked, "Do you 'know' this or is it just a gut instinct.

Cocking her head to one side, Catherine looked smug. "I'm not sure that I want to tell you, it might spoil the surprise."

But when he sprang into action, tickling her ribs until Catherine could no longer bear it, she called for a truce.

"I'll tell you. I'll tell you," she laughed and sighed and wiped away happy tears. "If I'm right, and I'm pretty certain that I am, we are going to have a lovely little girl – just one – and her name will be Katy."

Sitting back on his heels, Logan stared down at her as if she'd given him his greatest wish. He was going to have a daughter, and her name would be Katy.

"What a woman you are!" Logan was overwhelmed

and happy and giddy at the prospect of having a daughter. "I wish we could tell dad, but I'm just not sure."

"Let's at least wait until after the hospital appointment, then we'll decide what to do and who to tell."

Yes, very sensible, very typical of Catherine.

Sloane had been in touch after he and Frank had gone to the perp's location and found him gone, the news had been a bitter blow but today was another day and they had to put all that behind them and move on.

"Ok, so what's the plan of attack?" Emma asked Catherine after making the morning coffee for them both.

"Either I, or you, will keep monitoring his computer and track his new location," Catherine stated, quite unperturbed by yesterday's unsatisfactory turn of events. "There's no point doing anything else – to dwell on the fact that he got away will only add a negative layer to the investigation."

"Well aren't you the chirpy one today," Emma frowned, not feeling at all chirpy after Sloane had filled her in on the non-arrest of the perp.

Catherine actually laughed and had Emma looking at her for signs of hysteria. "Are you feeling alright – really, you're scaring me?"

"I am absolutely fine – never felt better." *And later on, when I'm sure my 'feeling' is correct, I might even share the reason why.*

All she could think was, 'Katy – my little girl's name will be Katy'.

Work was difficult, despite her upbeat mood. Catherine was so distracted and caught Emma covertly watching her.

Logan had gone in to work this morning, he had a meeting to sell off the construction side of his business and had sounded hopeful when they spoke this morning.

"My senior men have come up with a buyout plan," he'd told everyone at the breakfast table. "From what Terry, my top foreman, has told me already, it sounds like a viable offer."

His father had been less sure – management buyouts were notoriously poorly funded and required a very generous discount on the owner's part.

But Logan hadn't been put off. "If Terry, and his boys, can put up a reasonable offer, I'm not averse to helping them along a bit," Logan had smiled, watching his father roll his eyes at him.

"But you've worked hard to build that company – they'll already be getting a boost just by the fact that it has such a good reputation and a full order book. You shouldn't hand it to them on a plate, son," Henry had stated firmly.

"Well, we'll see, dad," Logan had placated. But

Catherine had known full well that he would do as he thought right. As she had given away her own company, CompuSafe, she could hardly criticise Logan if he all but did the same.

His workers had served him well and faithfully, if Logan wanted to give them a leg up by accepting a low buyout offer, then more power to him, Catherine thought.

CHAPTER FIFTEEN

When Logan appeared in the office that afternoon, smiling like a man who had a world of treasures in his pocket, Emma looked at him and frowned.

"Not you too – what's going on, Catherine's been smiling to herself all morning," Emma told Logan, her expression quite serious. "It's not normal!"

He had to laugh, was unable to contain his joy any longer. "We have a lot to be happy about – two lovely boys and another baby on the way – we couldn't ask for more."

They turned at the door just before leaving and saw Emma frowning deeply. She heard them laughing after closing the office door behind them and vowed to get to the bottom of it when Catherine returned.

"I'm so nervous," Catherine confessed as they travelled to the hospital in Logan's Range Rover.

"Why – worried your prediction might be wrong?" he chuckled happily.

Looking concerned, Catherine nodded. "You seem so overjoyed at the thought of us having a girl – what if I am wrong – what if we find out we're having another set of twin boys?"

Letting out a bellowing laugh, Logan reached across to pat Catherine's knee. "If it turns out that way then you'd better be prepared to have at least one more – we'd be one short of a five-a-side football team, else."

She couldn't believe it, her husband was a loony-toon! *Perhaps Emma was right, perhaps Logan is verging on hysteria? Well, we'll soon see how happy he is if it does turn out that I'm carrying twin boys. Oh Lord, how the heck would we manage, and I'm not so sure that Logan was joking about the five-a-side football team!*

The maternity unit was packed with women whose bellies were swollen with child. It scared Catherine just to look at them, but Logan was smiling quite happily.

Again she thought of what Emma had said and decided to keep an eye on Logan.

A little boy with sticky fingers and a half-eaten rusk in one hand, strode over to Logan and tugged on his trousers. "I'm going to be a big brother – mam said we're having a girl and I'm to look after her."

The little boy, who looked to be about 3, was so proud

of being delegated to look after his almost little sister that he apparently wanted to announce it to the world.

Everyone within earshot turned a smile on him and Logan took the hand without the rusk and shook it, making the little boy giggle.

"That's a very big responsibility," Logan told him. "I'm sure you'll do your job really well."

The boy's mother reached into a bag and handed Logan a wet-wipe. "I carry these everywhere – sorry if Carl has messed your trousers."

Taking the hand wipe, Logan used it and gave the woman a smile that seemed to dazzle her. "My trousers are of no consequence, your son is a credit to you – quite the little man."

She blushed and nodded, "Thank you," then sat back down, pulling Carl onto her knee.

"Hell, I really need to pee," Catherine whispered to Logan as she crossed her legs. "They tell you to drink loads then say you have to hold it all in until after the scan – bloody torturers the lot of them!"

Logan looked sympathetic, "I'm sure they only say that because it's necessary. Remember the boys, you were bursting then too, and look at the lovely images we got."

She couldn't help smiling – holding the boys before they'd left out had swamped her in motherly love. If the scan showed that she was, indeed, pregnant with twins, boys or girls or one of each, then she would be happy about it. Catherine was finding out that loving children was so much easier than she'd imagined.

Having Logan in her life was no doubt rubbing off on her and Catherine marvelled at her good fortune still.

There wasn't a day went by that she didn't thank heaven that they had found each other, that Logan had, by some miracle, loved her almost instantly.

The fact that he continued to love her even after they had begun to live together had flummoxed her for quite some time. She'd even told him so, wondering why he wasn't getting fed up with her taciturn moods and telling her to sling her hook – it's what she'd expected, after all.

But Logan had only laughed, hugging her to him and telling her that a few moods weren't going to get rid of him.

"Mrs Sayers...?" a voice called out, the woman holding a medical file in her hands as she looked about the waiting area for someone to acknowledge her.

"That's us," Logan stood, holding out a hand to Catherine when she looked startled up at him.

Reaching out, she took his hand and felt it gently squeezed. "I was miles away," she admitted.

"Not worrying, I hope?"

"No, thinking about the boys," she smiled.

"Good. Now let's see what the next one will be."

The nurse held the door open for them and took the medical file into the room and put it in front of the doctor.

"How are you doing, both…" the doctor greeted them with a curious half smile, "…I hadn't expected to see you again quite so soon."

Catherine felt her cheeks heat and Logan again gave her hand a reassuring squeeze.

"We enjoy the boys so much we decided we couldn't wait to give them a brother or sister," Logan lied easily.

The doctor raised a brow, looked from Logan to Catherine and then back to her medical notes. "I see you carried well – no problems during the pregnancy and an uneventful birth," he pronounced, satisfied.

"Can't say I agree with that," Catherine scoffed. "I consider giving birth to twin boys very eventful."

Logan chuckled and this time raised her hand to his lips. "Very," he agreed, and they shared 'a moment' as they looked into each other's eyes.

"Quite so," the doctor said after clearing his throat to bring their attention back to him. "Now, if you wouldn't mind laying on the examination table…" he indicated to his left, "…I'll just examine you before we do the scan."

He palpated Catherine's stomach very gently and smiled, "Nothing unusual there. Now I'll get our Sonographer and she'll carry out the ultrasound scan."

Logan moved to stand next to Catherine and took her hand. "It's hard to think another baby is growing in there – you're abdomen is virtually flat."

"That's because you've been a slave-driver in the gym," Catherine told him. "Now you'll have to take it easy on me."

The doctor returned with the Sonographer in time to hear the last comment. "Exercise is good for pregnant ladies – just don't use heavy weights or put excessive strain on your abdomen."

"Hi, I'm Ellie..." the Sonographer introduced herself, "...and I'm going to do your scan. Would you like an early photograph?" she asked kindly.

Logan and Catherine had looked at each other and smiled at hearing the young woman's name – a good omen.

"We certainly would," Logan beamed, like the doting father he was.

"Ok – I know you've had a scan before but I'd like to carry out a vaginal scan as you're so early on," Ellie explained. "Would that be alright?"

"You're going to scan my vagina?" Catherine asked wide eyed, then laughed when Logan and Ellie stared at her open mouthed. "Gotcha!"

With a nervous chuckle, Ellie got the vaginal probe ready and asked Catherine to draw her feet up towards her bottom and let her knees flop open.

"Very dignified, I don't think," she frowned up at Logan, but he just gave her hand another reassuring squeeze.

Then they were both watching the monitor as moments later the Sonographer pointed out their baby.

"It tends to look like a diamond ring," she smiled. "And it's blinking, so you already have a heartbeat."

"That is amazing," Logan sighed, his eyes glued to the tiny blinking light on the monitor.

"Is that really the baby…?" Catherine wasn't at all sure of what she was seeing.

"It is," Ellie assured her. "And I'd say you're about 6 weeks along…maybe 7."

"Six weeks…" Logan repeated dazedly.

"And you're sure there's only one," Catherine asked, her eyes searching the monitor for another blinking light.

"Absolutely. You had twin boys last time, I gather, but this little one is one on her own," Ellie smiled.

Logan and Catherine looked at each other – the Sonographer unaware of her slip.

"But there's no way of telling the sex of the baby just now, is there?" Logan asked cautiously.

"No, sorry, I just don't like calling a baby 'it', so tend to say him or her in a general way at this stage," Ellie told them.

"But there is definitely only one?" Catherine asked again, feeling an absurd sense of being short changed.

"There is definitely only one – were you hoping for another set of twins – girls maybe?"

Catherine looked up at Logan and smiled ruefully.

"You know, I think I sort of was," she told him, and felt her bottom lip tremble quite unreasonably.

Logan said just one word. "Katy."

When Catherine smiled it put the light of happiness back in his eyes and was reflected back at him in Catherine's.

"You've already been thinking about names?" the Sonographer asked with a chuckle.

"This one didn't take much thinking about," Logan said, bending down to kiss his wife full on the lips.

On the drive home Catherine was subdued and thoughtful, and Logan left her to settle with the news they'd just been told at the hospital.

"End of July, beginning of August – that would be very close to the boys' birthdays," she murmured without realising that she'd spoken out loud.

"That means we get to have a huge bash every year," Logan declared happily.

"What?" Catherine turned to Logan with a confused frown over her eyes.

"Well, it would make sense wouldn't it – celebrate the

children's birthdays with one big bash," Logan grinned.

"I...yes...I suppose you're right."

But Catherine wasn't smiling, in fact she felt horribly close to tears.

When he realised how upset Catherine was, Logan pulled over to the side of the road, switched off the engine and unfastened both seat belts. Then he pulled her into his lap and held her in his strong, comforting arms.

For endless moments they didn't speak and Logan kissed the top of Catherine's head while she wept.

"I know it's ridiculous, we didn't even want twins, but I feel like I've lost one, like there should have been two," Catherine hiccupped into Logan's shirt.

"But the dream..." he reminded her, "...you were so sure that Katy was one on her own."

"I said I was being ridiculous," Catherine snapped, then apologised quickly. "I'm sorry, I have no idea what's got into me."

"I think you'll find it's called hormones," Logan chuckled as he stroked her back. "You had the weepies last time, remember?"

"Oh hell, I did didn't I – I'd better not start blubbering all over the place – what a bloody show up that would be!"

<u>CHAPTER SIXTEEN</u>

Henry and Linda were pleased to hear the news that everything was going well with Catherine's unexpected pregnancy.

"They reckon I'm at least 6 weeks along, maybe 7," Catherine told them. "And there's definitely only one this time." Though no one spoke up, it was obvious that Catherine was having a problem with that part of her news.

If they had spoken up she couldn't have explained it — the dream had clearly shown only one child, a girl named Katy. But, maybe she had hoped that another little girl was sat somewhere out of sight or having a sleep, maybe.

She just couldn't shake the feeling of loss that the scan had brought upon her, as silly and irrational as it was.

"How about a nice cup of tea and a biscuit?" Linda offered, already getting to her feet. She got a nod and a smile from Henry and Logan, and a very reluctant nod from Catherine. She really would have to get to the bottom of what was wrong.

Minutes later, Linda came back with a tray of tea and a plate of chocolate-chip biscuits.

Even the sight of her favourite biscuits didn't bring a smile to Catherine's face, her expression distant, thoughtful and pained.

"I spoke to Caroline today," Henry offered, and Catherine seemed to come out of her trance at the sound of her sister's name. "Said she'd be delighted to oversee the refurbishment of the old ballroom – told her it's been shut up for years but she wasn't at all put off," he chuckled happily. "Really liked the idea of having our first family Christmas party there – probably come up with a lot of good ideas for it, knowing your sister," he chuckled again.

When Caroline had refurbished the wing that Catherine and Logan now occupied, along with the boys and Linda, Henry had gotten to know her very well. Had enjoyed Caroline's company and her enthusiasm.

"I really ought to call her, we haven't spoken since the barbecue," Catherine mused distractedly.

"That was only a few days ago," Logan reminded her.

She looked blankly at him then nodded as she realised what he had said. "Yes, but it seems longer."

"Why don't you go and give her a call now?" Logan suggested, hoping that it might bring Catherine out of her mood. "And don't forget to speak to Adrianne or you'll only feel guilty for leaving her out."

Getting up, Catherine at least remembered to take the mug of tea that Linda had made her and gave a brief wan smile to everyone around the table.

When the breakfast room door closed, Linda asked, "Whatever has gotten into her – was there more news from the hospital than Catherine told us?"

Heaving a sigh, Logan placed his mug of tea back on the table and shook his head. "She's been like this since we had the scan, very weepy and sad."

"But there's nothing wrong with the baby…?" Henry asked, desperately hoping for good news.

"No, nothing they found at this stage anyway," Logan sighed again. "Catherine had a dream…" he began to explain, "…one in which she saw us with a daughter, Katy."

Henry's smile brightened considerably and then he frowned. "But that's good, isn't it?"

"Yes…" Logan replied cautiously. "But when she saw the scan, saw only one baby, Catherine suddenly felt bereft – she said she felt like she had 'lost' the other twin."

"Aaahh," Linda breathed out, nodding her head in

understanding. "What you have to realise is, Catherine is an identical twin herself – her twin had twins – she had twins – the thought of having a single child never really hit home until she saw the evidence of her own eyes, and they were disbelieving."

"Disbelieving…but Catherine said she didn't see how we would cope with another set of twins – she seemed happy at the thought of having just one baby, a daughter, Katy," Logan told them, confused exasperation causing him to shake his head in wonder.

"On the surface, maybe," Linda told him. "But I think, subconsciously, Catherine had assumed it would be twins as that is what she's come to see as normal."

"So…what can I do to help her?" Logan asked.

"Your suggestion to call her sister's, and particularly Caroline, was a good one," Linda assured him. "Let's just see how she is after her chat."

It was almost knocking off time when Catherine went up to the office but Emma was still busy on her laptop.

"Hey, how'd you get on?" she asked when Catherine closed the office door behind her.

"Good," Catherine answered, not wanting to expand on her answer with the gory details.

"Oh, right. So, are you having one or two – or three," she added with a laugh.

But Catherine didn't join in. "Just the one."

Feeling unsure of the ground she was walking on, Emma decided that offering a cuppa was a safe bet. "Want a cuppa – I'm making?"

"No, that's alright, I just had some tea," Catherine replied, opening her laptop and burying her head in it.

Emma knew when there was something wrong with Catherine, she also knew when to back off and give her friend room to mull things over – this was one of those times and Emma went back to her work without saying another word.

Half an hour later Emma's mobile rang. "Hi," she said in greeting. "You are – ok, I'll be there in just a minute." Closing down her laptop, Emma got her jacket and walked over to Catherine. "Sloane's here, I'm going to get off."

"Ok. See you tomorrow," Catherine replied, not looking up.

Emma hesitated but decided to leave well alone. *But if you're not back to near normal tomorrow I'll brow beat you until you fess up!* "Bye."

Catherine wasn't working on the Christine Wakelin case anymore – not unless Emma asked for help. She'd taken over monitoring the perp's communications but hadn't seen any sign that the computer was back in use.

Sitting back in her seat, Catherine looked up at the ceiling, relaxing in the silence and isolation. It was nice to be alone sometimes.

The little girl was giggling, she looked to be about 2 – but this little girl had brown eyes and chestnut hair – she was the female image of Logan.

The tears were sharp and stung her eyes as Catherine laid her head in her arms on the desk. She was going insane, she just knew it. First the girl had looked just like her, now she looked exactly like Logan, and still there was only one girl in the dream.

What the hell was the dream trying to tell her? Or was it just that, a dream and nothing more?

But if that were true then the first dream might also mean nothing at all. Now Catherine was feeling thoroughly confused, and thoroughly pregnant!

Logan was right, she was hormonal – Catherine could all but feel them swimming around in her bloodstream and into her tear-ducts that simply wouldn't stop leaking tears.

She fell asleep at her desk and didn't hear Logan enter the office. He stood tall and muscly with a goofy happy grin on his handsome face. He watched her and sighed with the happiness that flooded through him whenever he thought of Catherine – but seeing the dried tears on her lovely face troubled him.

What could he do to bring her out of this...mood was the wrong word, but Logan couldn't think of anything more appropriate. He was worried about her, wanted to see Catherine as happy as she had been that morning.

Her face had been a wonder to him, smiling in her sleep and tears, that he was sure were due to happiness, rolling down the sides of her face.

She was his miracle, the boys she had given him were precious to be sure, but Catherine was his miracle. He would do anything to see her happy again.

He'd been about to give her shoulder a gentle shake when he heard Catherine say something in her sleep.

"No, Ellie, don't hit Andrew, he didn't mean to break it," Catherine murmured. But he'd heard it, Logan had clearly heard Catherine calling someone Ellie, and it sounded as though she'd been telling her off.

Now what, are we going to call the baby Ellie instead? This dream stuff is really confusing – I just wish I could see what's going on in your head.

Logan watched and listened a moment more, but when Catherine said nothing else he woke her gently.

"Come on, sleepy head," he smiled when Catherine lifted her head. "Dinner is ready," he told her as she stood.

But Logan didn't move, simply slid his arms about her and pulled Catherine into a warm embrace. "How are you feeling?" he asked as her arms lifted to circle his waist and her cheek snuggled into his broad chest.

She yawned then said, "Alright," though it didn't

sound convincing.

"Have any interesting dreams?" he asked cautiously.

"I…no," she said eventually. "None that I remember."

He wondered if she was keeping secrets, or if Catherine really didn't recall the dream with Ellie in it.

<u>CHAPTER SEVENTEEN</u>

Gathering up his tools the shadow put them in the van he'd retrieved from their old location. When he came back inside Christine was sat in a chair waiting for him to bind her to it with duct tape.

She didn't like it, he knew, but it was safer this way.

When he'd finished, he told her, "You be good now and don't make a sound. Not even if anyone should come to the door."

He hadn't used tape over her mouth since that first time she'd pleaded with him not to, and she'd behaved so he didn't bother this time either.

"I might be gone a while – got further to travel tonight." He didn't know why he told her, except that she was so childlike and he didn't want her to panic.

He was after a bad'n this night – a man of low morals as well as living the life of a street rat.

The shadow had watched him, saw him leave an ally after raping a woman and had followed him back to his hidey-hole. He'd take his time with this one – just like the man who'd taken his Mary had.

He'd vomited violently on hearing the woman in the alley trying to fight the street rat off. And when he'd punched her in the face to silence her, the shadow had wondered if the man who took his Mary had done the same to her.

She'd been black and blue, her clothes torn to shreds, and left for dead in an old cemetery.

She'd died alone – doctor said she hadn't died from her injuries, though there were many of them. Mary had died of exposure, unable even to crawl to find help.

The bastard used her and left her there alone – she would have been scared of the dark and being in a cemetery. Maybe this is the one that did it to her – but if not, he deserves to die like all the others. Rats spread disease – they must be exterminated!

The snatch was quick and clean – the shadow was getting really good at his job and no one noticed a thing.

He hadn't snapped this one's neck – the shadow had plans for this one. He drove a long way, pulled off the road onto a dirt track and into a grove of trees.

He hadn't seen a house for miles, it wouldn't matter if the street rat screamed. *He didn't care when that woman screamed... had tried to fight him off her.*

Slinging the unconscious man over his shoulder, the shadow moved into the darkness and became one with the night. He was in his element.

Tied to a tree, bound hands and feet, the street rat gradually woke and began to struggle against his trusses. His mouth wasn't covered and he shouted for help.

"There's no help for you here," the shadow told him. "Just like there was no help for that woman you raped in the alley."

The street rat quieted, stilled as if to make himself disappear, but the shadow watched him and smiled.

"Maybe it was you who raped my Mary," the shadow spoke from the darkness, the street rat unable to make him out. "Maybe it was you who beat her to a pulp, broke her legs and tore off her clothes," the shadow continued, but the street rat remained still and quiet.

"Was it you who left her to die all alone?!"

The first blow came out of nowhere, a branch hitting the bound man upside his head. It left him reeling and begging for his life.

"Please...it wasn't me...it wasn't me...don't kill me...please...don't kill me."

The shadow felt no pity, no hesitation in what he was about to do. The next blow to the head was so hard the street rat passed out cold.

Ripping off the unconscious man's clothes, the shadow beat him with his bare fists, wanting to feel the man break as he pounded his flesh.

When he'd done, the shadow sat in silence catching his breath – it was hard work teaching scum a lesson.

He waited, his breath visible in the frigid air as he hugged his black coat around him.

A moan rose into the night, a movement causing the beaten man to gasp in pain. "Please…" He didn't know what he was pleading for, the street rat only knew that he was dying.

It wouldn't be long now – the shadow watched and waited, never uttering a word of comfort.

There had been no one there to offer his Mary comfort – she had died cold and alone, desperate and afraid. This man could count himself lucky that death would come quickly – the cold, if not his injuries, would finish him off soon enough.

Once he'd rid a body of any possible identifiers the shadow would usually leave it in no particular position. But this time he lay the man out, spread eagled his arms and legs and carved 'RAPIST' into his chest with the sharp knife he'd used to remove the finger pads.

Detective Sloane Shivers had spent the day telephoning round all of the police stations within a 100 mile limit. His boss had an idea that the like crimes data bank had been tampered with, and if Sloane's findings were anything to go by, he was right.

Emma was on the same trail – she'd found 16 similar crimes, though not all were identical, but she hadn't been able to simply pick up the phone to get her information.

Catherine was still out of sorts, so Emma had got on with the search on her own. Now she would pin up all the printouts she'd made of the photographs on police files.

When she got up, Emma saw that Catherine didn't even appear to notice the movement as she normally would, so lost in thought was she.

Moving from the printer to the whiteboards, Emma worked methodically, putting dates and area information alongside each of the photographs.

When Catherine eventually did look up, Emma was standing back to assess her work, looking for any anomalies.

"That's where he started losing it," Catherine stated, and made Emma jump, she had moved so quietly.

"Christ, you gave me a fright!" Emma had a hand covering her rapidly beating heart as she regarded Catherine. "You've been quiet today – you doing alright?"

As if she hadn't heard a word Emma said, Catherine moved to the boards and pointed to one photograph in particular. "See how this one has bruising around here and here…" Catherine pointed to the side of the face and the left side of the ribcage, "…he was rougher, his temper got the better of him."

Squinting, Emma moved forward and examined the previous victims' photos. *Catherine's right, none of these victims have any bruising – but isn't that odd in itself?*

"These victims were likely killed at the moment they were taken," Catherine continued, walking to study the boards and photos more closely. "By the angle of the heads, I'd say most, if not all, had their necks snapped – that could indicate a member of the armed forces," she went on.

"Jesus…I never thought of that!"

Watching as Catherine continued to study the photos, Emma was amazed to see her get out a magnifying glass and look even closer.

"What are you looking at?" Emma asked, moving closer to Catherine.

"The wounds on these first few victims were inflicted after death – whereas these…" Catherine moved up the line of photographs, "…were all inflicted prior to death. Another sign of our perp's escalation."

"How do you know that?" Emma asked, looking at the wounds again.

Catherine pointed at the first few victims. "There's no blood around these wounds – the heart had already stopped beating when they were inflicted – whereas these…" she pointed to all of the victims including and after the one with the bruising, "…have blood clearly oozing from the wounds, therefore the heart must still have been beating when they were inflicted. But why…?"

"Maybe he simply got bored with offing them and getting no 'thrill'," Emma mimed exclamation marks in the air as she spoke.

"That's probably part of it," Catherine nodded. "But I think there was something about this victim that made him angry…something that has continued to make him angry with all these other victims," she speculated.

"I think I'll give Sloane a call, see if he's found anything more out about my case," Emma frowned, reaching into the front pocket of her jeans for her mobile.

Moving to the drinks area, Catherine stuck the kettle on and got a couple of mugs out. Emma rarely drank tea so she made a mug of coffee without asking. Catherine stuck to a mug of Lady Grey, the tea her sister had started her drinking.

She sighed, it had been lovely talking to Caroline and Adrianne, but she had deliberately kept her troubles to herself, deciding that they had enough of their own without her adding to them.

Still feeling bereft at some imagined loss, Catherine put a protective hand over her stomach.

We'll be fine. Mummy will get her act together by the

time you're born – promise.

Having put her tea on her desk and Emma's mug of coffee on hers, Catherine gave a little wave to catch Emma's attention, as she was still talking on her mobile, and mouthed the words, "Back in a minute."

Checking the nursery and finding it empty, Catherine continued on and down the stairs to the breakfast room.

"Ah, there you are." Grandad had a little boy on each of his knees and was singing 'Gee up Neddy to the fair' while bouncing them up and down.

Both boys turned at the sound of her voice and the smiles they gave her gladdened Catherine's heart.

"Sometimes I miss them so badly, even though I know they're just down stairs," she admitted, bending to kiss each little boy in turn.

"And that feeling will only get worse now that you're expecting again," Linda told her as she came in from the pantry. "It's just nature's way of preparing parents for what's to come; your instincts may go into overdrive until they settle down again."

"It's so difficult to do the right thing when you have two babies. I naturally want to give one of them a cuddle but don't want to upset the other one by making him wait. And maybe they'll become resentful, if I don't remember to take it in turns with who gets a cuddle first."

Catherine sighed and looked at her children longingly.

"I bet other mums don't get flummoxed by such simple problems – I'm such a moron in the family department."

Her arms felt empty and her heart felt like lead – how was she ever going to learn what seemed to come naturally to Adrianne and Caroline?

"That simply isn't true," Henry told her sincerely. "Adam and Andrew smiled the moment they heard your voice; if they were unhappy with you they wouldn't be twisting themselves up to see where you are."

"I suppose," Catherine sighed. Andrew put his arms out to her, obviously wanting to be held. Just as she'd taken Andrew in her arms, Adam decided he wanted to be held too. "Now what do I do, they don't do this when Logan's here."

"Not to worry," Henry told her. "I'll distract Adam and after a while we'll swap."

Singing gee-up-Neddy again, Henry soon had Adam enjoying himself as he bounced him on his knee.

Andrew lay with his head on Catherine's shoulder and snuggled into the side of her neck. He felt so warm and smelled so good, her hand rubbing gently over his little back as she swayed on her feet.

Now her heart was filled to bursting with a love she hadn't known herself to be capable of. *I'm so lucky, and so scared that I'll muck all this up. I just want to keep you both safe and well, to help you enjoy being a child for as long as possible.*

Daddy will get the playground made for you, and we'll have fun sharing it with all your cousins.

Why she was feeling weepy, Catherine couldn't have said – she felt happy and content with her life – but when the tears began she hid them, turning her face into Andrew.

CHAPTER EIGHTEEN

It had been late when Logan got home, the meeting with his solicitor and the men who were putting together a buyout plan, a long and tedious one.

He'd looked in their suite of rooms and found no sign of Catherine. After asking Linda where she might be, Logan had headed to the gym and hoped that his wife wasn't doing too much on her own.

More usually, they would do a careful workout together, but he'd been gone a lot lately.

The sooner all this buyout business is settled the sooner I can start taking care of my family again!

He was relieved to find Catherine in the pool instead of the gym, and watched her while she swam.

Her pace was steady, not pushing herself but doing a lot of laps. It was like she was thinking about something rather than trying to burn off excess energy, which she often did in the pool.

Then, Catherine would push herself, striking through the water until whatever had riled her was out of her system. At least it was the lesser of two evils – Logan preferred to use weights to burn off a good mad or when he felt really out of sorts.

He'd deliberately encouraged Catherine to swim rather than use the gym since they had found out that she was pregnant again.

Was she really as happy about that as she said – or is that at the back of this thoughtfulness? Maybe she was just trying to please him – he'd made it pretty clear that he'd be over the moon if they had another child.

At least it's just the one this time – though, maybe that's what's troubling Catherine. She's been like this ever since the scan, I don't know what to do to make things right for her.

He got up without Catherine ever being aware that he'd been there, then Logan went into the changing room and pulled on some Speedo's.

Waiting for her to do a turn at the end of the pool where he was standing, Logan dove in beside Catherine and kept pace with her.

She couldn't have missed the fact that Logan had entered the pool, yet Catherine barely missed a stroke and continued doing the front crawl for another 5 laps.

Now Logan really went for it, knowing that Catherine was watching him. Now that he'd started swimming he was enjoying pushing himself.

His hands cut through the water, his heavily muscled arms pulling his fine body along at an impressive speed. This was his element, it was where he had always been able to shine. And he'd found its cathartic properties useful over the years.

During his mother's illness, and after she'd died, Logan had spent long hours at the exclusive gym he'd been a member of and used its pool every day.

His mother and father had been a superb couple — they'd argued as most couples do, but more than anything else they had supported and loved each other.

If he could emulate their marriage in his own, then he would achieve something to be proud of.

There were never enough ways to say I love you to Catherine, but he must have tried all of them at one time or another - he would spend the rest of his life telling her and making her believe it.

When he finally came to where she was sat by the side of the pool, Catherine watched as he hauled himself out not bothering to use the steps as she had.

His body was so toned, so fine to look at as Logan strode to her and took the soft robe she held out to him.

"Thanks."

His smile had the power to stop her heart, and it did so now as he took a seat beside her at the poolside table.

She didn't know what gods had been looking down on her the day she met Logan, but she would be forever grateful to them.

"I got us a drink — you looked like you needed a stiff one so I got you a whisky," she told him, and he picked it up taking a restorative sip.

"It was a necessary but very tiring day," he told her, smiling wanly. "But I think we managed to iron out a deal that the men can afford — not that my father would be pleased at what I let the business go for."

Sipping at her iced orange juice, Catherine smiled. "You built that side of the business up yourself, it's not like you're selling your father's work short." Reaching out, she took his hand saying, "And, I for one, can't wait till you're working with us — I really missed you today...I seem to miss you all the time, these days."

Raising her hand to his lips, Logan kissed her fingers and looked deep into her tender blue eyes. "I love you, Catherine — more than I can say. Let's get showered off then go up and see the boys."

He got to his feet and gently pulled Catherine to hers, then put an arm across her shoulders and pulled her into his side as they walked.

They used the wet-room rather than the separate

stalls and Logan set the jets to hit them from all sides. The streams were just strong enough to massage the skin and warm enough to relax them.

When Logan pulled her back into him, Catherine leaned against him loving the strength and feel of his body. When his arms came around her, Catherine tilted her head to one side as he lowered his lips to the side of her neck and worked his way up to explore her sensitive ears.

He felt her bottom push back into him as Catherine arched and Logan moved his hands up to cup her wonderfully full breasts. Her moans were like a drug to Logan, the more he heard the more he wanted to hear.

When one hand slowly circled her stomach, Catherine felt it clench in anticipation. She knew just where those magic fingers were headed and slid her feet apart to accommodate them.

She was so hot and ready for him, Catherine's moans reached new heights when just one long finger entered her to stroke and tease.

"Logan…please…"

Her knees were weak and would have buckled had Logan's strong arms not taken her weight as he sent her flying over the first peak.

Turning her in his arms, Logan took her mouth and ravaged it. She was drowning in her love for him, for the way he could always make her feel – so precious, so wanted and needed. As impossible as it was, Logan loved her and worshipped her body in ways she could never have imagined.

If he didn't take her soon she would be reduced to begging...in fact...

Catherine took the shockingly hard length of him in her hand and stroked him while looking Logan right in the eye. "I want this inside me right now or I won't be responsible for my actions...got it!"

Without a blink of hesitation, Logan lifted Catherine off her feet and held her against the wet-room wall, then he plunged into her as she wrapped her legs around his waist.

She screamed, her head falling back as the sudden climax raced through her and clamped her body around him like a vice.

He thrust home again and again, driving her up and even higher than before. "Now, Catherine, now!" Logan demanded hoarsely.

She felt his whole body clench and ripple as he plunged into her and stayed buried deep as he emptied himself with a mighty roar.

They stayed entwined and breathless for endless minutes, his broad chest heaving as he held her to him.

"Christ, I daren't move," Catherine murmured into his

shoulder. "I don't think my legs would hold me up."

"I've got you," Logan's dark brown voice told her, his arms holding Catherine securely against him.

When they got around to actually washing, Logan offered to help Catherine and they ended up going another round. By the time they went up to see the boys, they were well sated and so clean you could almost hear them squeak as they walked.

Catherine was careful to pick Adam up first, mindful to take it in turns. "You are getting so big – you're both going to be as tall as your daddy."

Logan was beaming at both his sons, then looked long and lovingly at his wife. "You've given me so much, I wish I had the words to tell you how much you mean to me, Catherine – how much I love you and in so many ways."

She felt her eyes tear up to hear the words, and her heart tripped on a beat as Catherine smiled up at him.

"We've given each other the very best that our lives have to offer – now I'm looking forward to enjoying all of that with our children. When are you going to start on the playground?"

"Soon," he told her, and gave Andrew a quick tickle in his ribs. The little boy giggled happily, squirming in Logan's arms. "I've sourced a lot of the equipment already and I've asked Terry and the lads to do the work."

"That sounds great – at least you know the workers

and trust them to do a good job," Catherine added.

They each sat in a rocking chair and played with the boys on their knees. "Just look at how strong their legs are already," Logan told her, Andrew pushing up to stand on his daddy's legs.

Adam was doing the same on Catherine's legs and her grin was full of pride. "You'll be walking in no time," she told the baby. "But don't grow up too quickly, I want to enjoy snuggling my babies."

"You know, I bet they'll be walking by the time you have the next one," Logan suggested, smiling when Catherine looked shocked by the thought.

"That'll keep us busy," she said eventually. "In between feeding and changing a new born, we'll be chasing these two imps around the place. I'm exhausted just thinking about it," she told Adam, and blew a raspberry on his round tummy making him giggle loudly.

CHAPTER NINETEEN

Working in the office early the next morning, Catherine was surprised to hear Sloane Shivers' voice along with Emma's as they approached the door.

"Hey…" Emma smiled when they entered the room, "…did you get an early start?"

Catherine smiled and nodded. "Yep – I've been looking over your missing person's case and think I've found something interesting."

She watched Sloane's eyes narrow and silently congratulated him on not voicing his concerns about her methods of finding that 'something interesting'.

"What have you got?" Emma crossed the room to Catherine's side and read what was on her laptop screen.

"Jesus, Catherine, you really think this is connected?" Emma frowned at the screen and then at Catherine. "This happened 100 miles away – and just look at the way the body has been mutilated, not to mention the obvious posing. Our man doesn't go in for any of that."

Having moved to look over both women's shoulders, Sloane read the case file details and looked at the pictures that Catherine had opened in a split screen view.

"I'm not so sure," Sloane narrowed his eyes and continued reading. "I've found quite a few in outlying areas. I don't believe our perp operates in a specific area. In fact, I'm pretty sure he deliberately casts his net wide so as not to attract attention."

Looking over her shoulder at him, Catherine found herself smiling at Sloane – not an everyday occurrence.

"Let's pool our information," she suggested, and pushed back her seat to go with Emma and Sloane to the whiteboards to pin up the latest information she had just printed out.

"Ok, what do you have?" Catherine asked Sloane.

"Like you, I found a lot of cases where the perp had dumped bodies over a 50 mile area – but I expanded my search area to 100 miles," he grimaced at the memory. "I basically had to call all the stations within that perimeter to find what had clearly been wiped from our 'like crimes' database." He sighed and frowned, "We need to look at how he got into our files and at least try to block his access from now on."

Catherine merely quirked an eyebrow up and kept her

thoughts about how successful she thought he would be with that to herself.

He saw her expression and Sloane's frown deepened, but they seemed to have an unspoken truce going at the moment and neither wanted to break it.

Emma hurriedly stepped in to add her contribution to the discussion. "Apart from the excision of the finger pads, what makes you think this is our perp's work? He's not the only one out there doing that."

"No, he isn't, but I think this is the next step in his escalation," Catherine replied patiently. "In fact, by the amount of time he must have spent with this victim and the degree of escalation in the mutilation, I'd say this one is telling us something about why he's on this crusade."

"Crusade?" Emma asked, not sure she liked the emotive description. "Seems to me he's just a murdering bastard that gets his rocks off killing people!"

But Sloane was already shaking his head, agreeing with Catherine yet again. "No, there's definitely a mission at the back of these killings – we need to find out what that is and then we'll find our man."

Walking to the beginning of the photographic line-up, Catherine walked Sloane through what she had concluded so far. "These were all killed prior to mutilation – I think he snapped their necks at the moment he abducted them and carried out the mutilation at the dump site," she added, and got a nod from Sloane. "We also thought that might indicate a past association with the armed forces."

When Catherine came to the first victim to be mutilated while still alive, she stopped and considered her words carefully. "I believe this one was a landmark – he was the first one mutilated while still alive and I think there was something about him that pushed the perp over a line. Depending on whether or not the victim was conscious throughout the mutilation, he may have moved on to torturing them."

Sloane moved in for a closer look then nodded. "A worrying thought, but there may be a clue in there somewhere. Could be the date was significant, or the place where this victim was snatched from. Either way, I believe you're right about this one being a landmark case – I'll take all the details and follow up on that."

"I'll print you out a copy of everything we have," Catherine offered helpfully, and Sloane nodded his thanks.

"I agree with everything you've said so far..." Emma stated, "...but I still don't see how you connect such a diverse MO with our man – it's too extreme a deviation."

As the one who was still on a Private Investigator Course, Emma felt she had to voice her concerns based on the learning she had already had.

"We're taught that, although there may be some

deviation in each act of murder, the basic MO rarely changes – and this is way off," Emma stated, waving a hand towards the new photo that Catherine had pinned up.

"Not really," Sloane disagreed quietly. "You're being blindsided by the horror of the mutilation and the dramatic, undignified posing. But the basic MO has remained the same, in that he abducted this man and obliterated his identity. The rest is a drastic escalation, I grant you, but the basic MO remains the same," Sloane insisted a little more forcefully.

"Maybe." Emma conceded ungraciously.

"Anyway…" Catherine stepped in before a lover's spat could erupt, "…I'll give you a copy of this information also, and if you find the connection maybe you could let us know…ok?"

"Will do – same goes," he added, knowing that Catherine and Emma would be digging even deeper into this case.

They finished up by comparing the victims that Emma and Catherine had found and the ones Sloane had managed to unearth. Information was shared and set them on a level playing field, ready to move on and catch the murdering bastard!

Time passed so fast, Catherine was surprised when Emma reminded her of the time. "You'll miss being with

Adam and Andrew for their dinner if you don't go down now," she urged Catherine.

"Ok, I will if you really don't mind," Catherine said as she logged off her laptop and got up to go.

"I've brought a lovely seafood salad with me – you go and I'll take a break too," Emma smiled encouragingly.

When she went downstairs Catherine got a lovely surprise. "Logan – when did you get home?"

He was sat next to his father on the settee in the breakfast area of the kitchen diner. Henry had Adam and Logan was throwing Andrew up in the air.

His excited little screams caused Catherine some anxious moments, but she sat at the dining table without saying anything.

But Henry had noticed her discomfort. "My son never drops the ball," he said, reminding her of Logan's rugby reputation. Then he chuckled when Catherine's mouth fell open. "I was joking, Catherine."

"Oh, ok," she smiled, but was glad when Logan settled Andrew more securely on his knee. "So, how come you got home so early?" she asked Logan.

"It's all done – contracts have been signed and I am officially a free man," Logan grinned happily.

"Y you…you…" she couldn't find the words, her heart and mind were tugging in opposite directions.

She was glad to have him join her at work, to have

him by her side on a daily basis – she'd missed him so much recently. But would he really be happy – her brain was trying to figure that out and wasn't coming up with a good enough argument to convince her that he would be.

"You did this for me," she told him simply.

He could read her like a book – Catherine was going to blame herself if this didn't work out. But Logan was determined that it would work, he would make sure of it.

"I did this for us," he corrected her gently but firmly. "My family will always come first, Catherine."

Her bottom lip trembled and she had to bite down on it and pull back the threatening tears.

Handing Andrew off to Linda, Logan put an arm around Catherine and steered her towards the back door.

Thankfully it was mild for the time of year and her jumper was enough to keep Catherine warm. That and Logan's lovely body heat as he pulled her into his side.

They walked round the side of the house and off towards the lake that Lakelands had been named for.

"Are you having second thoughts about me becoming a partner in the business?" Logan asked, referring to the investigations agency Catherine and Emma had started.

When she didn't answer immediately, Logan felt his heart sink. "Ok, well, there's plenty around here to keep me busy and maybe I'll start up another business from home – something small."

"What...no, what are you talking about?" she demanded when she realised what he was saying.

"You're obviously not keen on taking on a new partner, I should have realised before," Logan smiled wanly, but gave her shoulders a reassuring hug. "But I'll keep myself busy, and no doubt the boys will take up a lot of my time."

"Logan, I don't have a problem with you working with me and Emma," she looked up at him and stopped walking. "But you gave up everything for me, everything you and your father took years to build up – what if we're not enough? What if we start arguing and...and..."

She sucked in her bottom lip to stop its tell-tale trembling and willed her unhappy tears not to fall.

He looked down at Catherine and shook his head. "I'm not going anywhere, Catherine," he told her. "We are going to grow old together – do you believe that?"

She nodded, then shook her head and the tears finally fell. "I want to, I really do. But this is all too perfect," she told him, her arm swinging out to encompass the house and grounds in her statement. "Someone like me doesn't live happily ever after. I'm a foster kid who learned that I'd better stick up for myself because no one else would. And I'm good at it, I can take care of myself in my own world – but this world is so new and so perfect..."

It was no good, how could she explain the insecurities

of a foster kid to a man who had grown up surrounded with so much love and security in a home as lovely as Lakelands.

She looked across the lake to the little shack that his mother had used as a painting studio...and could hardly believe her eyes.

Ellie was sat at her easel in front of the shack and painting the beautiful lake, as she often had before she'd died. And then she lifted her head and smiled directly at Catherine, even giving her a little wave.

"Catherine?" Logan was anxious now, she hadn't heard him talking to her and now she looked completely blank, as though seeing something that he couldn't.

"Catherine?!" he said again, this time louder and more firmly. It took another few moments, but Logan saw the change in her expression when she came back to him. "Are you alright? Did something happen?" he asked, thinking what a stupid question that was. Of course something had happened, but he hadn't a clue what.

Then Catherine smiled and it blew right through him.

"Catherine...?" he said again, only now his voice was gentle and curious.

"Your mother has never left you," she told Logan, smiling at him like she was giving him the best news ever. "Ellie still enjoys the island and the shack – she still paints and looks very happy."

"You just saw my mother?" If Logan hadn't already been aware of Catherine's special 'gift' he would have thought this a joke in very poor taste – but this was Catherine and he knew her talent was very real.

"She smiled and waved at me," Catherine told him, her smile now wondrous at Ellie's happy greeting. "I think she wanted me to know that she's here for me too. Do you think that's what she meant?" Catherine looked up hopefully at Logan.

"I've told you before, my mother would have loved you, Catherine. Maybe she realised that you wouldn't believe it until she told you herself," he grinned, and chucked her under her stubborn chin.

"She's beautiful, Logan. Even more so than the photos you have in the house." Catherine put a hand to her stomach and walked to the edge of the lake. "We're having another baby, Ellie – I hope you'll look in on us."

From her seat in front of the easel, Ellie nodded and waved, smiling with happiness before fading from view.

"I wish I could see her too," Logan said, looking across the lake to the little island that his mother had loved. "It was so hard when we lost her, my father almost broke under the weight of his grief."

"And you were the rock that pulled him through it," Catherine put a hand on his arm then hooked it through and hugged Logan. "I think I sensed that about you," she told him. "You're so strong and reliable, so unshakable in everything you think and do. I feel safe with you, Logan." Putting a hand to his cheek, Catherine had to stand on her tip-toes to touch her lips to his. "I feel safe and loved. I'm sorry I don't always show it, or know how to, but I love you with all my heart, Logan – that will never change."

CHAPTER TWENTY

Sloane Shivers was doing what all police detectives did, he was slogging through information and following up on leads and hunches.

He'd looked more closely at the victim Catherine had pointed out to be the first one mutilated while still alive.

A sure sign of anger and escalation – but what was it that pushed you over that edge, Sloane asked himself as he stared at the crime scene photo's stuck on his office wall. *Did this victim remind you of someone – someone associated with a past tragedy? Or is it something else about him that got to you – or maybe it's the date that mattered, did something happen on that same date – was it the reason you began killing in the first place?!*

His cop gut told Sloane that he was on to something. *And then we have this man – you've never mutilated any of your other victims in quite this way. Did you choose him because you knew he was a rapist...or does he represent a rapist that did something bad to someone you love...loved?"*

Looking through the autopsy record for the first significant victim, Sloane made a note of the Pathologist's estimated date and time of death.

Ok, so maybe we're looking for a rape victim on that date sometime in the recent past?

He looked at the map where he'd marked out all the known victims' dump sites. Then he put a large red pin in the centre of it and decided to look for rape victims within a 10 mile radius of that point.

It felt like he was getting somewhere at last, even if it was just to eliminate another theory – not that he had a lot of them. Cases like this fascinated him, but Sloane also found it frustrating when the puzzle pieces just refused to fit together.

Much as he didn't like it, the information that Catherine and Emma had gathered had been particularly helpful. He hadn't found the victim with 'rapist' carved into his chest, and he might prove vital to cracking the case.

He was learning to bend a little, where Catherine and Emma's investigative techniques were concerned. As his boss, Frank had, Sloane was beginning to understand the higher motives behind the illegal computer hacking. And that was the sticking point that he was gradually allowing to bend – it was illegal.

She might drive him crazy with her antics, but Emma had gotten under his skin and now he couldn't think past her. His life would be empty without her – though he only admitted that to himself.

But they had talked about starting a family. Well, he'd told her that they ought to get a move on as neither of them were getting any younger…and that much was true, wasn't it?

Still, maybe he should have asked her to marry him first. But hell, did anyone really do that anymore?

Giving himself a mental shake, Sloane got his head back into the game and began a computer search for the rape victim he was sure was at the centre of his case.

Back at the CCSI office, Emma had come to the same conclusion and was trying to fit the pieces together. The PI course that she was still taking, gave her some pointers, but this was the real world, not some tidy case-study.

One thing you can count on, the real world is anything but predictable – people do the craziest things for the craziest of reasons, no rhyme or reason to it.

"I'm looking at rape cases going back 5 years from the time of the first victim," Emma told Catherine when she brought her a mug of coffee over. "I doubt he started killing immediately after whoever it was, was assaulted or murdered-"

"Assuming there is a 'someone' who was assaulted or murdered," Catherine broke in. "We don't know for sure that that is what tipped this man over some edge or other – he may believe he had an epiphany from God, for all we know."

Emma just looked at her, tipped her head to one side and said, "You're not a happy bunny this morning, take a seat and tell Aunty Em all about it."

Frowning deeply, Catherine took the seat across the desk from Emma and sat staring into her tea.

"Do you think you and Sloane will ever have kids?"

Brows raised and her mouth gaping, Emma sat back in her seat – that had been nothing like what she'd been expecting Catherine to say.

"I...have no idea," Emma replied, caught off guard. "Why do you ask?"

"Being a mother scares me to death," Catherine admitted out of the blue. "I mean, the kid doesn't ask to be born, has no choice but to burst out into a world it knows nothing about and may not want to be a part of when it does find out how crappy it is."

Emma was grimacing badly, "That was so gross – you made giving birth sound like a scene from Alien. And when did the world become such a bad place – just because we see and hear a lot of sick, depraved things, that's our job not our lives, Catherine. I, for one, love my life and am glad to be a part of this crazy world."

"You are?" Catherine looked surprised.

"Honestly, Catherine," Emma sighed. Are you saying you're not – you have two incredible little boys and a gorgeous man mountain that came down from heaven just for you...sounds pretty damned good to me?"

A protective hand stroked over her stomach as Catherine thought about the daughter she would bring into the world next summer.

She looked at the boards and the ugly things that one man had done to so many seemingly innocent people.

"I watched my mother die a horrific death, saw the terror and agony she suffered at the hands of a sadistic maniac – now I'm bringing a little girl into this chaotic world and I'm scared for her." Not taking her eyes off of the carnage someone else had wreaked, Catherine added, "If anyone does to my daughter anything like what happened to my mother, they would be begging for death by the time I'd finished with them!"

Emma felt the chill of Catherine's words go right through her. But wouldn't she feel the same given what Catherine had witnessed at such a young age.

"You need to stop right there," she told Catherine. "What happened, happened, there's no changing that – but to allow it to hang over your life now is both destructive and meaningless."

When Catherine frowned at her, Emma added, "Remember your mother – was she a loving person, did she do her best by you, did she love you for everything that you were and not judge you for it?" Shaking her head in despair, Emma reached across the desk and took Catherine's hand. "As a mother, would you want your death to be the driving force in Adam and Andrew's lives – or would you want them to carve out a happy place with someone they love?"

Her bottom lip trembled and precarious tears hung on her lashes as Catherine gave the hand holding hers a squeeze. "Thanks for that. I know I'm not the easiest person to be around. I make Logan mad when I say life was easier when I was on my own, but what I really mean is, when it was just me I could get by day by day without fearing what the world would do to the people I loved. Now, I'm so scared, sometimes it's really debilitating. I want to lock the boys in this house and never let them leave it, never let the world near enough to hurt them."

"Yet you opened yourself up to love and all the complications that brings," Emma smiled. "The love of a father and two sisters you never knew you had – that took a lot of courage, Catherine. Logan is the icing on a very tasty cake – and the boys...don't get me started. If anything is guaranteed to bring out my broody side, it's those adorable little boys."

Smiling, Catherine felt the familiar joy in her heart that mention of her boys always brought her. "They are very special. I love them so much it hurts, but in a nice way."

"I think you need to go spend a few minutes with them," Emma suggested. "Cleanse your soul with their innocence and come back ready to dance with the devil."

After Catherine had gone, Emma called Sloane and shocked the hell out of him. Without any hi or hello, Emma said, "We should go for it. I love you, I know you love me even if you don't say it, so we should just do it, move in together and make a baby!"

"What-"

That was the only utterance Sloane got out before Emma was on him again. "Don't even think of having second thoughts, you're the one who suggested it in the first place. Just get your bags packed and move in this weekend – I'll be waiting."

He stood in his office staring at the mobile phone in his hand like it was a grenade about to go off. Sloane Shivers was not a man to be shaken easily, but Emma had rocked his world in a way no other woman ever could.

What the hell was that? She gives me my orders and then hangs up – what the fuck?

But he was smiling as he recalled Emma's words. 'I love you', she'd told him. It was the first time either of them had said the words and he was idiotically pleased that she had said them first.

Looks like I'm going to have a busy weekend, he grinned to himself.

Catherine had a very troubled weekend. Her nights were filled with disturbing cryptic dreams. The first one had been about Christmas again, and Katy had been giggling as Adam and Andrew played with her. As with the first time she'd had this dream, Catherine thought Katy was the child she was carrying, but then who was the little girl of around the same age who peeked around the Christmas tree and looked just like Logan?

The second dream had featured her family, including Katy, having the best Christmas ever – but sitting in a corner, all alone, was Ellie, the little girl that looked so much like Logan. Was she the daughter of a cousin of Logan's, is that why there is such a family likeness?

But why was she looking so unhappy and alone...unloved and lost?

She couldn't shake the feeling that Ellie was the child she had 'lost', yet Catherine knew it was extremely unlikely. She hadn't bled that she could recall – she hadn't had a period since the boys were born.

Logan did his best to pull Catherine out of her morose thoughts, taking her and the boys for a walk around the lake. "How's Emma's missing person's case coming?" he asked to get some conversation out of her.

"What…?" Catherine looked up at her husband, she knew he'd spoken but hadn't really 'heard' him. "Sorry, I was lost in thought, what did you say?"

Smiling ruefully, Logan repeated his question. "I was just wondering how Emma's missing person's case is coming on – any new leads?"

"Oh…err…no, not that I know of," Catherine told him, then realised that she really didn't know if Emma had made any progress or not. *I'm losing my grip, this isn't like me. I'll have to catch up with Emma on Monday, though I'm sure she would have told me if there had been any significant breakthroughs.*

Suddenly Catherine's mouth went into gear before her brain had a chance to and she blurted out, "Do you have any cousins or uncles or some relative that is expecting a baby?"

The complete non-sequitur had Logan coming to a sudden halt and blinking in surprise. "I have no idea," he began haltingly. "I do have cousins, but I don't know if any of them are expecting a baby in the near future – why do you ask?"

"Ellie – that's the name of the little girl I keep dreaming about – surely she's named for your mother?"

Logan gave that some thought and nodded. "It sounds probable – but why would you be dreaming of a little girl that some other member of my family is having?"

"I don't know…I have no idea…but she keeps showing up and I feel like I'm supposed to know why. It's driving me crazy," Catherine told him. "She looks so sad and alone – it tears at me, Logan – she looks just like you."

That brought Logan up short. "Like me? You think I'm having an affair?!"

Now it was Catherine's turn to get blindsided. "I'd never given that a moment's thought – are you telling me that you're having an affair?"

The boys were forgotten, but were luckily asleep in their pushchair. "Catherine, this is getting out of hand. I would never have an affair. You need to stop and think about what you're saying."

Staring up at him, Catherine could only shake her head, then she lunged at him, wrapping her arms around his waist and burst into tears.

He held her, stroked her hair and kissed the top of her head. "Catherine, stop now," he hushed her softly. "Don't cry, sweetheart – we'll get to the bottom of this."

"I hate myself – she's looking at me to help her, but I don't know how to do that."

They returned to walking round the lake, Logan with an arm across his wife's shoulders and holding her firmly to his side.

"I want you to confide in me Catherine, whenever you

have these dreams I want you to tell me about them —
ok?" Logan asked, trying to support Catherine in the only
way he knew how.

Nodding her head against Logan's side, Catherine gave
a long sigh. "I will, I promise."

CHAPTER TWENTY-ONE

The weekend had certainly been a busy one, just as Sloane had envisaged. He'd hired a van and a couple of willing officers from his station helped him to pack up his belongings and move into Emma's house at Lakelands.

"Cor-blimey, guv…" the younger officer gaped at his surroundings "…did you win the lottery or somethin'?"

Sloane shrugged and laughed. "In a manner of speaking, Benson." His eyes were looking at Emma when he spoke and he did indeed consider himself to be a lucky man.

It took a couple of hours to offload the small moving van, but Sloane had always lived light so there were no major problems fitting his belongings in.

Later that Saturday evening, Sloane and Emma sat snuggled up together watching a film, but around 9 pm Sloane suddenly started to yawn and Emma took the hint.

Switching off the television, she stood and held a hand out to Sloane. He took it and she pulled him to his feet with a sexy smile on her lips.

"Let me show you the rest of the house," Emma offered, her voice low and sultry.

Going willingly, Sloane allowed himself to be led up the stairs and into the bedroom.

"Let me take that shirt off, then I can show you where to hang it up," Emma smiled while her fingers got busy with his shirt buttons. When she'd removed it, Emma went over to a wardrobe that she had cleared for him and, sure enough, took out a clothes hanger and hung up the shirt.

Turning back to Sloane, Emma looked at his broad bared chest with nothing short of hunger in her eyes. But she kept up the game for a little while longer.

Moving forward, she popped the button of his trousers, slid the zipper down then slipped them down his legs and told Sloane to step out of them.

He did so and after hanging them up, Emma turned back to Sloane with a lascivious grin.

"You finished showing me around?" Sloane asked, his smile indulgent, a brow lifted.

When Emma ran her hands over his broad chest, she followed them with her lips then said, "You've seen the house, now I'm going to show you the perks of moving in."

Before she could say another word, Sloane lifted her off her feet and Emma landed on her back on the bed with Sloane straddling her.

"You're working too hard…" he grinned down into her shocked face, "…let me take over for a while."

First she'd screamed in surprise now she screamed because Sloane was doing things to her body that drove Emma wild.

If this was a taster of things to come, Emma was all in favour.

When she met up with Catherine in the office on Monday, Emma was walking on air with a constant smile on her lips.

"Did you make any headway on the Christine Wakelin case?" Catherine asked, eyeing Emma cautiously.

Frowning, Emma looked at Catherine with some concern. "I told you about the alarm he triggered…don't you remember?"

It was Catherine's turn to frown, she had a vague recollection of some such conversation, but it was very vague. "Just go through it for me again, would you."

"Ok, well, Friday morning I got a hit on the spyware monitor I've got running on his computer – if he logs on to any network I get an alarm show up on mine." Emma grinned, she liked this part of her job – she may not be up to Catherine's level of computer excellence but she could hold her own with 'ordinary' people.

"And he logged on?" Catherine's eyes went wide. "Then why didn't we get a location? Why didn't Sloane and Frank go after him?"

Catherine was devastated, how could she have been told such important news and not remember the conversation?

"It was too brief – like he was testing the water," Emma told her. "But I'm hoping he'll get sloppy – nothing bad happened when he logged on so maybe he'll log on for longer next time, then we'll be waiting."

Nodding, Catherine gravitated towards the coffee making area, lost in thought. She'd been developing a new programme, a mole that could relay its location in real time the instant the host turned on their computer. It did a hell of a lot more than that, but that was the function that Catherine was hoping would pay off for them on this particular case. Finding the murdering creep was imperative to saving the lives of any future victims he'd already picked out.

"I'll need to install a new programme onto your laptop," Catherine told Emma while she made them both coffee on autopilot, her mind lost in thought. "When this case is finished I want to make some modifications to it – I've already done mine and it's better than ever, much faster and a lot more secure...with a few added features."

"You want to modify my laptop…?" Emma eyed Catherine dubiously as she handed her a mug of steaming coffee. "I don't let anyone tamper with my baby, she's sensitive and just how I like her."

But Catherine barely heard her protests and continued to outline the changes to Emma as if she hadn't spoken. "The mole I've developed will infiltrate any system that attempts to infiltrate ours. It not only mines data it gives us remote access to the host computer and feeds back a real time location of that computer. It also morphs, looks like one thing when it's really another – we can control what that is as and when we need to."

"An auto-bot then," Emma proclaimed knowledgeably. "They've been around for years – what's so different about his one?"

"I'll take you through it as I install the programme, it'll be easier that way," Catherine told her.

Walking back to her desk, Catherine missed the annoyance that flitted across Emma's face. She'd been on cloud 9 until now, constantly reliving the many ways she and Sloane had celebrated his moving in with her, all of them imaginative and extremely satisfying.

Now it was back to reality and the world of murder, missing people and corporate espionage.

Catherine had just closed a case of corporate espionage – turned out it was a fellow executive in a fashion emporium that was selling information to a competitor. His computer had contained all the information Catherine had needed to follow his trail back to the competitor.

Gambling debts and an expensive mistress had pushed him to take the duplicitous actions that had cost the fashion house dearly.

"By-the-way, Logan's desk will be arriving sometime today – this afternoon, I think," Catherine announced.

That cheered Emma right up. "Great, when does he start working with us?"

"Not till next week – he's still tying up the handovers," Catherine grimaced, not liking the idea of all the meetings that Logan needed to attend. "The building side is easy enough – he's known his men for years and the buyout is an amicable one. The Estate Agency business is another matter – the buyer is a pain in Logan's arse, so he's a pain in mine too!"

"And mine if he's what's holding Logan back from joining us," Emma declared loyally.

Catherine actually laughed at that, and Emma realised the strain her friend was under. "With everything that's going on right now, you must be feeling the strain?"

"I'm alright," Catherine brushed Emma's worries aside. "But what about you, didn't you say Sloane was moving in – don't suppose he's had time to get under your feet yet?"

Grinning, Emma waggled her eyebrows at Catherine suggestively. "Can't say he managed to get under my feet, but we assumed every other position," she laughed, and laughed even more when Catherine blushed.

"You're so easy to wind up," Emma continued.

"And you just love doing it," Catherine berated her, though not with any feeling. "I just hope this is not a sign of things to come – Logan will not want to hear all about your nasty sex life when he finally moves in here!"

"Nasty! Nasty!" Emma pretended outrage. "I can assure you not one moment of our marathon house christening was in the least bit nasty. I thoroughly enjoyed every moment of it!"

"One more word about S E X and I'll come over there and stomp all over you," Catherine threatened. "Then you can tell lover-boy that you got under my feet!"

"That would be assault…" Emma grinned "…and 'lover-boy' just happens to be a cop, so…"

One look at Catherine's face told Emma to shut up and get back to work, so she shrugged and put her head down but continued smiling.

Moments later she was on her feet again, "He's on, he's working…the bloody murdering bastard is online!"

Crossing the room quickly, Catherine stood at the back of Emma's chair and watched her go to work. Her fingers were like rapid gunfire as they punched the keyboard.

"Don't lose him!" Catherine warned. "Christ, I wish I'd had time to install the mole programme, we can't let him get away again!"

"Get on the phone to the cottage, Sloane won't have left yet he's on a late shift!"

Spinning on her heels, Catherine crossed back to her desk and dialled the cottage. When Sloane's sleepy voice came on the line she got annoyed.

"Get yourself out of bed and over here – Emma's got the murdering bastard online and she's tracking his location as we speak!" She heard a groan as Sloane bashed into something and then an expletive that she would have used herself not so long ago. "Now, Shivers, not this time next bloody week!"

When she slammed the phone down and frowned over at Emma, Catherine could see that her partner wasn't impressed with her telephone skills.

"He's on his way," she told her, and crossed to make Shivers a mug of coffee by way of conciliation.

Only minutes later Sloane stood in the office having pelted down the driveway into the main house and up the stairs to the office.

"What's going on – have you got him?" he panted.

"If I'm right – and I really think I am – he's still in Upper Stanton," Emma proclaimed almost disbelievingly.

"Would he really be that brazen?"

"It's actually a good strategy, if you think about it," Catherine put in. "Most people, like yourself, would think he'd get the hell out but staying put is a less obvious plan."

"And I think it was a plan," Sloane observed knowledgably. "He didn't just slink away into the night and disappear the night he evaded us – he had a bolthole to run to, a safe house, just in case we got too close."

"It looks like he's using a library connection," Emma continued after a bit more probing. "I think that brief logon he did on Friday has given him confidence that we can't find him now that he's moved. I don't think he's quite so computer savvy as we've given him credit for."

When Emma looked up from her laptop, Sloane was already on his mobile to his boss and partner, Inspector Frank Harper.

"Yes, the library in Upper Stanton," Sloane confirmed. "Good idea, I'll meet you there – I'm leaving now," and Sloane looked to Emma in case there was any more information he needed to impart before he put his mobile back in his pocket.

There wasn't. The murdering bastard was still online and Emma was able to see every move he made on his laptop. "I'll carry on following his actions on screen then I'll call you if I get anything usable."

"Just don't stop tracking him, and don't let him know that you're watching," Sloane said, and luckily left the office before Emma could tell him just what she thought of his unnecessary advice!

"Who does he think he's talking to?" she asked Catherine instead. "I'm not some blundering idiot, I know what I'm doing!"

"Hmm, annoying isn't he?" Catherine chuckled as Emma glared at her. "And he didn't even touch the coffee I made him – oh well, I'll just have to drink it."

"Then you can make me one while you're up – this one is about cold," Emma grumbled ungraciously.

<u>CHAPTER TWENTY-TWO</u>

The local police were informed of the situation and sent officers to surround the library until Inspector Frank Harper got there to take charge.

When he arrived, Frank noted the two armed officers at the main library doors. He gave them a nod and went inside with a plain clothes police woman pretending to be everyday patrons of the library.

Speaking to the librarian in charge, they found out that the perp was using a student cubicle, a small room on the right hand side of the room.

The trouble was there were six such rooms, all next to each other and two others were also in use.

"Do you know which room the man is in?" Inspector Harper asked the librarian.

"Yes, he arrived first and asked for a private room with internet access to use his laptop in and I put him in cubicle 1, the other two are in 5 and 6 – the students prefer them as they're closer to the photocopier," the librarian informed him.

"Ok." Frank looked around and noted at least 20 other people in the library and asked the librarian to go to them and ask them to leave very quietly. "Once they're out we'll get more officers in and approach the cubicle to make the arrest," Frank told the female officer.

In the meantime, they moved closer to the cubicles to see if they could observe the man without drawing attention to themselves. They pretended to look at the small music library of tapes and CD's but were covertly watching the man through the glass partition.

"He's older than I thought he would be," Frank observed. "Must be in his late forties or early fifties."

"I'd say fifties," the police woman agreed. "A bit late in life to suddenly start murdering people."

"Indeed. There must have been something that triggered him – something traumatic that happened to either him or someone he cared for," Frank observed quietly.

"Maybe he got the sack from a job he'd been in for years – sometimes it's something as mundane as that that pushes them over the edge," the young police woman suggested.

"Hmm, you never know." But Frank didn't think losing

his job had caused this type of murdering rampage.

The man in the cubicle was absorbed in his work, not looking up from his laptop.

"Ok, is that everyone?" Frank asked when the librarian came back to him. She nodded but Frank said, "What about staff, did you get them out too?"

"There was only a couple of us on today — Laurie has gone out with the others and I'll follow as soon as you say it's ok," the librarian told him.

"Very good," Frank smiled. "You go out with the rest and, if you wouldn't mind, ask the two officers outside to come in please."

She nodded and left and moments later the two armed officers entered the small library. They had on bullet proof vests and took the lead as they all headed to the cubicle where the perp was still working.

In less than a minute the two armed officers had opened the cubicle door and swiftly stood the startled man up and put handcuffs on him.

"What's going on — this is an outrage!" But it was a token protest, one look at his laptop told the officers all they needed to know.

"So, you're researching your next victim," Frank observed after looking at the laptop screen and the medical records the man was altering.

The perp didn't say anything more, just stared at Frank defiantly.

"Take him to the Sheriton Police Station – I'll be there as soon as I can – I have a couple of errands to run first," Frank told them.

He looked at the laptop and the battery indicator – the perp had been using it plugged into the mains so the battery should be fully charged.

But Frank knew, from his own experience, that laptops constantly used on the mains often ruined the internal batteries and therefore didn't run for long once unplugged.

He didn't want to chance unplugging it only to have it shut down – as it was the laptop was unsecured and at no risk of being wiped by some failsafe programme that the perp might have installed for protection. But once it shut down a password would be needed to open it up again and that might lead to some big complications.

Taking out his mobile, Frank called Catherine.

"Frank, have you got him?" she asked before he could speak.

"Yes," he confirmed, and Catherine turned to Emma and punched the air triumphantly. "But I have a problem," Frank continued. "He was working on his laptop when we arrested him and it's still open – I'm loath to unplug it in case the battery doesn't hold a charge and the damned thing goes off, but I can't just leave it here."

"Hell, that was a stroke of luck," Caroline blew out a

breath. "Leave it plugged in and I'll be with you in an hour – Emma and I are on our way."

She turned to Emma and grinned. "You are now my assistant – I read in the small print of my consultancy contract that I'm allowed to have one, so you're mine. Now, let's get a move on before someone starts meddling with that laptop!"

Catherine turned her blue sporty car onto the motorway and sped along it past the turnoff to Sheriton. It was quicker to go to the next junction along and go directly to Upper Stanton.

In just under an hour they pulled up outside of the library and quickly went inside.

Frank was sat at a table nearby the cubicle drinking a cup of coffee that the librarian had provided him.

"Don't you look comfortable," Catherine smiled as she and Emma approached the inspector.

Frank shifted in his seat and put the cup down on a little table nearest him. "I gather the traffic was minimal..." he said, glancing at his watch "...you seem to have made excellent time."

"I'm used to the route now – I travel it all the time to see my sisters," Catherine told him.

"Is Sloane here?" Emma asked, looking around for the tall detective that had recently moved in with her.

"No, I asked him to go directly to Sheriton – that's

where the perp was taken," Frank explained.

"Ok, let's get down to business," Catherine stated, all professional consultant now that the pleasantries were over with. "Where's the laptop?"

Frank took them to the small cubicle and indicated for them to go inside.

"Did you touch anything?" Catherine asked, her eyes sharp as she looked up at Frank.

"Not a thing – just looked at what he was working on and saw it was a medical file," Frank told her. "By the looks of it he was in the middle of altering it."

Catherine nodded, half a sentence had been deleted and he must have leaned on the return key when he'd been surprised as there was a large gap after the deletion.

"Emma is going to take over from here," Catherine informed Frank whose brows drew together in confusion. "As a consultant I'm allowed to have an assistant – I read it in the fine print – so I'm allocating Emma as my assistant as this was her case in the first place."

"Hmm." It was a rumbling sound of dissatisfaction, but Frank knew that Catherine was right. It wouldn't be the first time that a consultant had insisted on using one of their own people to assist them, but he hadn't thought Catherine would be one of them.

He saw her as a take charge person, one who always wanted to take the lead and make sure that the job got done right. He hadn't expected her to pass the hat on to her partner, though Sloane had told him that Emma had some masterful computer skills of her own.

Emma gave him a pat on his arm as she passed Frank to take the seat Catherine had vacated.

Interlinking the fingers of both hands, Emma pushed them forward and cracked the joints making both Catherine and Frank wince at the sound it made.

"First off I'm going to change the password so that we can get this baby back to our office," Emma smiled up at Frank. "It won't matter if it shuts down then, as I'll know the new password to open it up again."

"It's that simple?" Frank asked sceptically.

"It is for me," Emma grinned. "We've been monitoring his computer and all his keystrokes – we've had his password for some time now, we just needed him to log on so that we could find him again."

Seconds later, Emma closed the lid of the laptop and unplugged it, noting that Frank looked vaguely ill.

"Stop worrying, we'll get this back to the office and you'll know everything that's on it in a matter of hours," Emma assured him.

He looked at Catherine and she nodded, giving Frank a reassuring smile. "Emma is brilliant – not as brilliant as me but that is only to be expected."

Emma and Frank looked at each other then burst into

peals of laughter. It was probably just stress that had them laughing so hard, but Catherine had an artless way about her sometimes and just said things as she saw them.

They knew that Catherine was referring to her genius IQ and wasn't disparaging Emma in any way. A fact was a fact in Catherine's eyes, and she was just stating the obvious.

She frowned as the two pulled themselves together and followed them out of the library to her car.

"I'll be in touch as soon as Emma's got anything for you," she told Frank, still frowning at his smiling face.

He straightened the smile and nodded, "Right you are, take care on the drive home."

Frank didn't know that Catherine was pregnant or at least, she didn't think he did.

"Has Sloane told Frank that I'm pregnant again?" she asked Emma on the drive home.

Looking surprised by the question, Emma said, "Why wouldn't he – you did tell everyone at the barbecue?"

"I suppose," Catherine frowned. "I just didn't expect it to become common knowledge so soon."

"Is that a problem?"

Emma was confused by Catherine's concern, was there a reason that she wanted to keep the pregnancy a secret?

"No." But Catherine didn't sound sure. "No…" she repeated "…it was just unexpected."

They remained quiet for the remainder of the journey, Catherine lost in her own thoughts and Emma left wondering what was wrong.

She determined to talk to Logan, knowing that he wouldn't misinterpret her concern for out-and-out prying.

When Frank got to his station house, he went straight to the interview room that Sloane had put their perp in.

"Has he asked for a solicitor?" Frank asked Sloane, who was standing outside the observation window watching the man.

"He hasn't spoken a word since they brought him in," Sloane informed his boss.

"Hmm. I gather you've cautioned him and told him why he's here?" When Sloane nodded, Frank said, "Get the file with all the photos in it and the information on the missing woman, Christine Wakelin - I need to do a couple of things in my office before we go in and question him."

The two men parted company and met up again half an hour later at the interview room.

"Have you got everything?" Frank asked before opening the door.

Sloane held up the manila file he was holding and said, "It's all in here."

Just before he opened the door, Frank said, "You take

the lead and go in hard."

They had worked together for a few years now – Frank had never been one to sit behind a desk and Sloane had learned a lot from the older man's experience.

Knowing his boss' rhythm, Sloane wasn't surprised when Frank pulled a chair out and sat quietly watching the perp, never taking his eyes off the man.

"You were cautioned when you were arrested, do you need me to read you your rights again?" Sloane asked as he stood straight backed at the end of the table.

The man remained silent so Sloane repeated them anyway, just for form.

"You do not have to say anything, but it may harm your defence if you do not mention when questioned something which you later rely on in court. Anything you do say may be given in evidence."

Formalities over with, Sloane slammed the manila file down on the table in front of him and flicked the front cover open. There, in full colour, was the gory photo of the first victim that they knew of. Taking them out one by one, Sloane slid them across the table in front of the still silent perp.

At first his eyes didn't move from the point they had fixed upon on the wall opposite him, but eventually they lowered to look at the photos.

His expression never changed, he looked at them as

he might look at a magazine while waiting in a dentist surgery, no more interest than that.

"Why?" Sloane snapped the word out and it rent the oppressive silence of the room violently.

The man went back to looking at the spot on the wall and didn't answer.

"Got a kink, haven't you," Sloane suggested, but didn't get a response. "Men or women, it doesn't matter to you – you like them both, don't you?"

He was deliberately inferring a sexual aspect to the crimes, yet no sign of sexual abuse had ever been found.

Sloane saw a twitch beneath the man's left eye and knew the slight had hit home. He decided to play that aspect up, if he could get a response, even a hostile one, Sloane knew he could begin to open the man up.

"What's the matter, you not getting any at home? Or maybe there is no one at home – maybe this is the only way you can get your jollies," Sloane sniped, and slid the photo of Ellen Fisher's naked body under the perp's nose.

Again, the nerve under the perp's eye twitched as he looked down at the photo and back to the wall again, but he didn't speak.

"She's a bit young for you – I bet she wouldn't have looked at you twice if you hadn't forced her," Sloane stated conversationally. "But why erase her background..." he saw the man move his head a fraction in the direction of his voice, and Sloane knew that he'd gotten his attention. "Yes, we know all about that, you left a trail a mile wide," he lied.

"That's a lie," the man stated calmly.

So, he was proud of his computer skills – didn't like being called sloppy.

Sniggering dismissively, Sloane leaned on the table bringing his face closer to the perp's. "We've got junior techs better than you – it was one of them who found you the first time when you managed to give us the slip."

His cheeks flamed as the perp became increasingly agitated, but he managed not to say anything else.

Sloane had spoken to Emma during the time his boss had gone to his office, and she had told him the password for the perp's computer.

"A bit amateurish to use your wife's name as your computer password," Sloane told him, watching the man for a sign to confirm that this had been the case.

His head whipped round and his eyes were blazing, "Don't you mention her name! Don't you dare speak it!"

Raising a brow, Sloane began leafing through the notes in the manila file and said, "Was she your first – was Mary Hellen your first victim?"

The sound of his wife's name seemed to send the man over the edge of reason and he lunged at Sloane.

The officer at the door immediately sprang forward

and restrained the man, telling him that he would be handcuffed to the fixed table if he didn't behave.

"You don't speak her name," the man demanded again, glaring at Sloane like he was scum of the earth.

"Ok…" Sloane nodded "…but only if you tell me about her. Where is she, did you kill her too?"

He watched the man's bottom lip tremble then saw the moment when he steeled his emotions and drew them in. "My Mary was murdered, but not by me. The likes of you did nothing – nothing!" he yelled, angry again now.

"And you thought that gave you the right to do this!" Sloane picked up the photo of Ellen Fisher and wafted it under the man's nose. "She had family too, people who cared about her just the way you did about your wife. What gave you the right to snuff out her life, to erase her as if she were nothing?!"

The man went silent again, looking back at the wall and just folded his arms across his chest.

He'd hoped the man's anger would trip him up, but that seemed to be a futile hope now. Sloane, however, was a patient man, he would grind him down until the man eventually confessed.

For the next two hours he rubbed the man's nose in the murders, spelling out all the wicked acts that had been performed on them and adding a few in to taunt him.

The man only rose to the bait a couple of times, and even then he hadn't said anything incriminating.

"Would you like a cup of tea?" They were the first words Frank had uttered and the man seemed confused by them. But Sloane wasn't, he'd seen this act before and knew when his boss was taking over the questioning.

Turning in his seat, Frank waved the uniformed officer forward and then turned back to the perp. "Would you like milk and sugar?"

They could have been ordering tea in a restaurant the way Frank smiled over at the confused man sitting across from him.

"Yes, two sugars please," the man told the officer.

"What about you Detective – tea or coffee?" Frank asked pleasantly.

"Make mine a coffee, black no sugar," Sloane growled, as if he was annoyed by the interruption.

"So, that's two teas with sugar and one coffee," Frank smiled up at the officer who nodded and left the room. Frank spoke the officer's name and the time he left the room for the sake of the tape, then he turned back to the perp and smiled.

"Now then, tell me about your wife – what exactly happened to her?" He kept his voice quiet and the tone sympathetic, as if he were offering comfort to a friend.

The man just looked at him at first, then his body

seemed to relax into his chair a little.

"My Mary was an angel, she went out of her way to look after people even though she was always in pain," the man recalled quietly.

"In pain?" Frank prompted when the man didn't go on.

"She had arthritis, caused her a lot of pain no matter what the doctors gave her – nothing eased it for long."

"And was she out looking after people when she was murdered?"

The anger was back in the man's eyes, like a light it switched on and burned brightly. "The bastard dragged her into a grave yard, raped her and beat her so badly she couldn't even drag herself to the street to get help. And you lot did nothing, not a bloody thing!"

The man's voice had gotten louder as he'd recounted his tale, and Sloane had cautiously moved forward in case he lunged across the table at Frank.

"I'm sorry for that," Frank said sincerely, and watched as the man eyed him sceptically. "We don't always manage to catch the criminals, but that doesn't mean we don't try."

"You could have caught him if you'd wanted to badly enough – you've got all kinds of things, like DNA, that you can use to find them," the man growled angrily. "You just didn't give a damn, she was nothing, not worth the time and trouble to the likes of you."

"I'm sorrier than I can tell you that you feel that way," Frank sighed. "You lost the woman you obviously loved very much and we didn't liaise with you closely enough to assure you of our efforts. In that much, we most certainly did fail."

That Frank was admitting to any kind of failure seemed to confuse the man even more, but he also seemed to sense the sincerity of his words.

"Certainly our methods of investigation have improved markedly over the last few years – how long ago did your Mary die?"

CHAPTER TWENTY-THREE

"Jesus!" Emma was shocked at what she'd found on the laptop taken from the library. "We've only scratched the surface of what this maniac has been doing."

"What do you mean?" Catherine asked, looking up from a pile of paperwork she was sifting through.

"I mean, he's documented everything – not photographically, but he's written down every detail from start to very bloody finish," Emma explained.

"What about Christine Wakelin, was she one of his?"

Emma frowned, skimmed through the files dated around the time Christine Wakelin disappeared and shook her head. "She isn't here. At least, her death record isn't here. He has a lot of research on her, as he has for all the others, but unlike those he doesn't have a description of the murder and the place where he left her body."

Emma looked up, truly astounded, and said, "I think she's still alive!"

But Catherine wasn't convinced. Why would a man who clearly had no empathy for his fellow man, or respect for human life, suddenly allow one of his chosen victims to live? And if he had, where was she? She hadn't gone back to her friends at the Salvation Army, they would have notified Emma if she had.

No, it was more likely that her body just hadn't been found yet and maybe the murdering bastard hadn't gotten around to writing up his little inventory of death yet.

"Don't get your hopes up," she told Emma. "Not that it wouldn't be nice to think that Christine is safe and sound somewhere, but it really isn't a likely scenario."

Catherine watched as Emma's hope died and felt guilty for pushing reality in her face. "Why don't you give Sloane a call, maybe he can use some of the information you've found during questioning. And maybe he can get the murdering bastard to tell them where Christine is?!"

Emma's face lit up as she pulled out her mobile. "I'll do that," she smiled, hope rising again. "I'm not giving up on Christine until they tell me they've found her body. I just have a gut feeling about this one!"

Catherine wondered about her own gut feelings – hers seemed to be concerned exclusively with her pregnancy just now. *Am I blocking again? If I am I don't know how I'm doing it – might be a handy skill to learn though.*

Wouldn't you think this damned gift would be a bit more consistent – hell, if you're going to have 'feelings' it would be nice if they came up with something concrete now and again!

Catherine suddenly thought of Fiona Richerson and her husband, the way she'd 'known' that the man who had taken their daughter and her boyfriend was outside their house, intending to murder Natalie.

He hadn't been able to stand the idea that Natalie and Josh had gotten away from him, so he'd raged and found the Richerson's house intending to take his wroth out on Natalie.

But Natalie hadn't been home, and instead he'd taken his rage out on her parents, slaughtering them before the police could stop him.

His anger woke me, I couldn't have blocked that amount of rage out even if I'd wanted to. He was pure evil!

She thought of Natalie and Josh and the wedding she'd attended with Logan. *They were such a lovely couple, devoted to each other and coping admirably with all they'd been through.*

Thank God Josh's parents took Natalie in after her parents' deaths. I think it was their kindness that helped to pull her through the worst of it, the rest was down to Natalie's own strength of character and Josh's love.

If anyone knew what the love of a good man could do it was Catherine. Her childhood trauma, actually witnessing the rape, torture and murder of her own mother, had twisted her up so badly that she'd been admitted to a psychiatric unit.

For 2 years she hadn't spoken a word – she couldn't remember now if it was because she couldn't or because she simply didn't want to, but suspected it was the latter.

She hadn't allowed anyone to get close to her emotionally, nor physically either. Catherine had been a virgin when she and Logan had become an item, and he had been the perfect gentleman.

It made her smile to think of her first time with Logan, the way she had taken him by surprise and impaled herself on him when he'd made love to her only to balk at taking her virginity.

Well I certainly took care of that little problem! Hell, what did he expect, he got me all worked up and then backed off at the final moment – chivalry is all well and good but that was taking it too damn far!

"You're smiling away to yourself, are you thinking of the boys...or Logan?" Emma asked with a wiggle of her eyebrows.

"Neither!" Catherine lied. "Did you call Sloane?" she asked to distract Emma.

"I did. He said he'd grilled the perp for over 3 hours

and barely got anything out of him – then Frank suddenly offers him a cup of tea and talks to him like they're having an everyday conversation." Emma chuckled at Sloane's description of the situation. "I think Sloane was a bit peeved that his methods didn't work, but he said it's just Frank's way, and the perp has really started to open up."

"Whatever works," Catherine dismissed. "What about Christine, did you ask him about her?"

"He's of the same opinion as you," Emma admitted. "But I told him to get confirmation or I wasn't going to give up. If Christine Wakelin is still alive she needs us to be looking for her!"

Pursing her lips and nodding her agreement, Catherine decided to say nothing more on the subject.

"How about some coffee – I could certainly use a cup," Catherine said as she got to her feet.

"Ok, thanks," Emma sighed, fed up that she was the only one who held out any hope for Christine.

CHAPTER TWENTY-FOUR

There was a knock at the interview room door and then a female police officer entered the room and handed Sloane a couple of A4 sized sheets of paper. He studied them then gave her the nod to leave.

"Mr Ferrier, we've found your wife's case and will be looking into the investigation to see if there's anything we can build on," Sloane told the man, who didn't seem to realise that he'd been identified. "It was particularly nasty, the way your wife was beaten and left to die – I'm truly sorry for your loss."

Ferrier didn't look convinced, though he wasn't as hostile towards Sloane as he had been. "You won't do anything, it's just words with your lot."

But Sloane didn't take offence – if a woman he loved had been taken in such a manner, and no one had been brought to book, no doubt he would be just as bitter and twisted as the man sat in front of him.

"I don't give my word lightly…" Sloane continued evenly "…but I'm giving it now – I will personally look into your wife's case, review all the information gathered and endeavour to find who took her life. That is a promise."

Ferrier looked from Sloane to Frank and back again after Frank nodded in confirmation. "I'll take your word and hold you to it – my Mary deserves to rest in peace and she won't for as long as her killer roams free!"

"Is that what you were trying to do?" Frank asked quietly. "Were you trying to put a stop to the man who did this to your wife?"

Looking sad and confused, Ferrier rubbed his hands over his tired face and shook his head. "I don't know anymore," he confessed, and Sloane smiled over at Frank.

This was it, Frank would gently probe and sympathise and Ferrier would spill his guts without giving it a second thought.

For the next three hours Ferrier took them through the gory details of his crimes.

He'd started killing on the first anniversary of his wife's death. Nothing had come of the investigation and he'd grown angry and vengeful.

"They told me it was most likely a vagrant, a tramp who was going to be very difficult to track down," Ferrier said. "And I started looking around – I'd never noticed how many of them there are, scroungers living on the streets and pocketing benefits to buy drugs with. It's not right!"

At times Ferrier became extremely angry, so volatile that the officer at the door moved uneasily. At others he was unnaturally calm, telling in detail of the way he'd abducted his victims and the routine that he went through.

Sloane and Frank were silently horrified to hear that their search had turned up only a fraction of the man's victims. He'd been moving around the country, basing himself at the centre of the homeless population and then 'exterminating' them, as Ferrier put it.

"Rats in the sewer of life," he'd raged at one point. "Vermin just waiting to pounce on the unwary. My Mary wouldn't have hesitated to help any one of them, and what did they do, they raped her and beat her, left her in a cemetery to die all alone. She would have been terrified," he sobbed, all the fight going out of him. "Terrified."

"Mr Ferrier, you haven't mentioned Christine Wakelin..." Sloane put in when Ferrier began pulling himself together "...what can you tell us about her whereabouts?"

"Christine...?" For a moment he looked dazed, confused, struggling to think clearly.

"Christine…yes…Christine…just a child really, not like those others. She looked after her mother, she's a good girl, not a bit like those others."

"So you took her in…" Frank suggested "…looked after her?"

"She'll be scared if I don't get back there soon," Ferrier said, not seeming to comprehend his situation. "And she'll need a meal – I'll get a Chinese take-away, she likes them."

"If you give us the address, we'll send a female officer to let Christine know the situation," Frank offered, being careful not to state the obvious that Ferrier would never be allowed to leave the police station.

"Not sure about that…" Ferrier frowned "…she won't be able to let them in and I told her not to talk to anyone that came to the house – no one!"

"Don't you worry, we'll make sure to send someone she won't be scared of," Frank smiled reassuringly.

It took another half an hour of reasoning for Ferrier to give up the address, but eventually he did so.

Frank handed the address to the officer at the door and instructed him to send two female officers, with backup, to that address to find Christine Wakelin.

"And warn them that she has some learning difficulties and may not understand what is going on – a softly, softly approach, understand?" Frank warned, and the officer nodded before leaving the room.

Turning back to Ferrier, Frank smiled and said, "There now, we'll make sure Christine gets a meal and is safe and comfortable. We're going to take you to booking now, then you'll be taken to a cell and a meal sent in for you. It's been a long day – I'm sure you must be hungry by now?"

"I suppose," Ferrier said, his tone disinterested.

"Mr Ferrier, I need you to understand that you are being arrested for the murders you have confessed to and that a Solicitor will be appointed for you if you do not have one that you prefer to use," Frank said quietly but firmly.

"I don't care what happens to me…" Ferrier sighed, his eyes dim with defeat "…but you do as you promised – you find the man who killed my Mary."

"I gave you my word and I'll keep it," Sloane told him.

It was late by the time Sloane returned to the cottage and Emma had fallen asleep on the sofa.

He sat in a chair watching her sleep and thought about what had happened to Mary Helen Ferrier. It didn't do to bring his work home, but in this instance he didn't seem able to shut it out.

Jesus, if this is what love does to you no wonder I haven't let it happen before!

It scared him half to death, the thought that he might

lose Emma. He'd never allowed himself to get that involved with a woman before, had always backed off the moment his heart started getting mushy.

But I don't want to back off this time, she's different from all the rest. But marriage…?

She turned on the sofa and Sloane moved forward to kneel on the floor beside Emma.

"Hey, sleepy-head, you'd be better off in bed than on this settee," he told her, and smiled when she opened her eyes to look at him.

"Oh…it's you…" she yawned, and rubbed the back of her hand across her eyes.

"Well, who else were you expecting?" he asked, not sure why he suddenly felt annoyed.

She frowned and yawned again, then smiled and leaned forward to kiss him. "Just you, sweet-cheeks."

It made him smile and Emma found herself drowning in it, he was so damned handsome!

"Did you get a confession?" she asked as he pulled her to her feet.

"Christ…and then some," Sloane sighed heavily. "We had no idea how prolific he'd been, and he just told us like he was reeling off a grocery list. It was tragic, really."

"I told you about the files I found on his laptop…" she reminded him, and he nodded "…well, I also found a Dropbox account – the files on his computer are just his documented kills for this particular year — he uploads them to Dropbox at the end of each year. Sloane…there are so many victims — I never dreamed there would be so many."

He guided her to the bed and helped Emma to undress. Kissing every inch of exposed skin, Sloane lost himself in the moment and washed away the grime of the day with love.

Every touch reminded him that there was beauty in the world, that they could give each other this no matter what happened outside of this room.

"I love you, Emma." It was the first time he had said it. "I love you, and I want you to marry me."

She would have sat bolt upright in shock, but Emma was pinned beneath Sloane's weight. Then he was inside her, moving gently, driving her up and over the crest of a wave that crashed right through her being.

She must have been dreaming — Emma tried to get her brain to work but Sloane was still moving inside her and his hands were doing exquisite things to her body.

"Did you…just…ask me…to marry you…?" she choked out, in between gasps of pleasure.

He leaned up and looked directly into Emma's eyes, bleary from the orgasm he'd just given her. "I did, but you didn't give me an answer."

Was he kidding, did he really expect her to make such

a life-changing decision while he was still driving her crazy?

She groaned and felt her eyes actually cross as Sloane circled his hips then plunged deeper into her.

"Yes! Yes!" she repeated, then lost all ability to think as he thrust into her, again and again, and her body shattered beneath him.

His roar of satisfaction came from deep within and encompassed much more than physical pleasure.

CHAPTER TWENTY-FIVE

"Can you believe the poor woman tried to fight the police off when they went to rescue her," Emma told Catherine in the office next morning. "Sloane said she told them to leave her alone when they tried taking the tape off her hands and legs, that Mr would be really cross with her if he came home and found her undone."

"I think he genuinely came to care for her," Catherine replied as she poured water into 2 coffee mugs. "They said she wasn't hurt or abused, just tied up when he left the house."

For a moment, Emma looked blank, then she rolled her eyes and said, "You've been reading the reports — when did you hack in?"

"Last night — I was restless so did another couple of hours after we put the boys to bed," Catherine smiled and handed Emma her coffee mug.

"I see Logan's moved his desk in," Emma observed with a grin. "Does that mean he'll be joining us on Monday?"

Pursing her lips, Catherine narrowed her eyes and said, "You can stop drooling all over my husband – you have a man of your own now!"

Emma leaned back in her chair and her expression became dreamy. "And what a man he is – I hope good sex doesn't stop with marriage, I'm not sure I'll go through with it if you say it does."

Raising her brows in shock, Catherine let out a snort of laughter. "Are you telling me he finally manned up and proposed?"

"I don't know about the 'manning up' part, Sloane has always seemed manly enough to me," Emma chuckled good naturedly. "But yes, he has proposed and I actually said yes."

At that moment the office door opened and Caroline walked in. "Hi girls, I've just arrived to give the ballroom a once over – I've got my work cut out there, I can tell you."

Catherine looked at Emma and jerked a thumb in her sister's direction, "Well, go on, you know you're dying to spread the news."

"What news – you're not pregnant too, are you?" Caroline asked looking delighted by the idea.

"One step at a time, Caroline," Emma laughed happily.

"We need to get married first – Sloane proposed last night and I accepted."

Grabbing Emma's left hand, Caroline's smile turned to confusion, "So where's the ring?"

"You're getting ahead of us again," Emma shook her head. "I don't think he planned to ask me last night – it was sort of in the throws…if you see what I mean."

Laughing with delight, Caroline said she definitely did. "So when are you going ring shopping? And when do you think the wedding will be – we'll have to get new outfits," she turned to Catherine, who paled visibly. "Now don't you give me any grief – I'm sure Emma won't want to see you wearing just any old thing to her wedding, and Adrianne will love the chance for a girly day of shopping and tea-cakes."

"Now see what you've started," Catherine hissed at Emma, throwing her hands up in the air. "Why does everything that ever happens around here end up in a shopping spree. We're the same size, damn it, just pick out something to suit the occasion – I don't really care if I go in a coal sack!"

"Well that's not very nice," Caroline turned to Emma. "I'm sure she doesn't mean it – and if she does it'll be up to her sisters to make sure Catherine doesn't shame you on your big day, and we won't let you down!"

"Shame-" Catherine had been about to give as good as

she was getting when Emma broke in, hands held up in a gesture for peace.

"Hold it…hold it…let's not start a war over something that isn't even happening yet," she told them quickly. "Sloane and I haven't even discussed a date, it could be in another year or two for all I know."

The twins turned to look at her in unison, both astounded at the prospect.

"I'm not saying it will be, just that it could be," Emma defended when the two women frowned at her.

"Maybe he's not really sure after all," Catherine suggested to Caroline.

"Hmm, or maybe she isn't – which is it?" Caroline demanded, both sisters taking a step closer to Emma.

"You know, you two are scary when you pull this double act," Emma told them, sitting as far back in her seat as it would allow.

The office door opened again and this time it was Logan who stepped into the office.

"Err…am I interrupting something…?" he asked, noting Emma cowering back in her seat with Catherine and Caroline hovering menacingly close by.

"No! Not at all," Emma snapped out before Logan could back out of the office. "We were just discussing weddings and shopping…and things," she tailed off lamely.

"Weddings – who's getting married?" Logan asked, smiling at the happy news.

"She should be…" Catherine jerked her thumb in Emma's direction "…but we were just wondering if she's already getting cold feet."

"I gather Sloane proposed – good man," Logan grinned. "When's the big day?"

"When indeed…?" Caroline echoed ominously.

"All I said was, we haven't discussed it yet and Caroline was discussing shopping for outfits and Catherine was about to have a hissy fit and then they both turned it around on me," Emma babbled quickly.

"Ahhh…" Logan said knowingly. "You showed them fear – a big no, no with these two – you've got to stand firm and let them know you won't be bullied," he stated confidently, then chuckled when the twins turned identical challenging looks on him.

"Your desk is over there…" Catherine pointed to the corner of the room between hers and Emma's desks "…if you came in to get set up do it quietly while we settle this."

"Sorry…" he shrugged in Emma's direction, "…she is the boss."

"Now what was that about a year or two – is he trying to get you to have a baby now on the promise that he'll marry you some day?" Catherine demanded, already pushing long thin needles into a mental effigy of Sloane Shivers. "That man has got some nerve!"

"He what?!" Caroline gasped hotly, not giving Emma a chance to confirm or deny the accusation. "Typical! Men want their cake and eat it too – you just tell him what he can do with his proposal and we'll back you up all the way!"

The twins turned to each other as the baby alarm in the boys' room told them that they were both awake from their morning nap.

"Oh, just in time to see the boys," Caroline clapped her hands together, forgetting to be upset on Emma's behalf. "Let's get them up and I can tell you my plans for the ballroom," she told Catherine as they left the office.

On a long relieved sigh, Emma leaned forward and banged her head repeatedly on her desk.

Logan laughed and said, "Tell me all about it – were they right about Sloane wanting a baby now?"

Sitting up slowly, Emma had her eyes closed and kept them that way until she'd taken a few calming breaths.

"Yes, Sloane does want us to have a baby. No, he isn't trying to get me to have one now and then marry me sometime in the future – that was Catherine's idea," Emma shook her head as if to clear it. "The two of them managed to get everything turned around – if they see Sloane before I do I swear they'll lynch him!"

"Why are you laughing?!" Emma asked when Logan leaned back in his seat and roared out loud.

"That's my Catherine," he stated happily. "She cares a great deal about you – if she thinks Sloane is trying to trick you into having a baby then renege on his marriage proposal...well...let's just say he'd better duck and run before she catches up to him, and Caroline wouldn't be that far behind either, by the looks of things."

"You know what, I'm getting out of here before they come back," Emma stated as she got up and pulled on her jacket. "I promised I'd let the Salvation Army know as soon as we had some news on Christine Wakelin – I think I'll take this opportunity to do that in person."

"Drive carefully," Logan waved as Emma hurriedly left the office.

So, this will be my new work station – I can't wait to get started. They certainly seem to take on some interesting cases. Catherine's industrial espionage case was quite something, until Emma trumped it with her missing person stroke murder case.

From what Catherine said, Christine will need a lot of care – not because of anything Ferrier did, but to help her over the trauma of her mother's death and her own limited ability to care for herself.

The streets are a dangerous place, as Christine found out for herself. I wouldn't wish that life on anybody.

Even before this case, Logan had always been generous to charities that took care of people – be they street people or those escaping domestic violence. He would make it his business to see how those charities were doing and would also look into the care of the mentally challenged living on the streets.

I suppose I'm as guilty as the next person of not looking too closely at a problem that's right under my nose. The Christine's of this world deserve better – I'm going to try to see that they get it...at least here in the Midlands.

<u>EPILOGUE</u>

The Range Rover pulled out of the Lakelands drive with Logan behind the wheel.

"Tell me again why we're going back to the hospital – I thought the next scan was at 20 weeks, I'm only 8 at the outside," Catherine complained.

"I told you, the consultant just wants to check you out," Logan said patiently. "He looked at the photos the Stenographer put in your medical file and he wasn't absolutely satisfied with them."

"But why wasn't he – that's what I want to know?" Catherine persisted doggedly. "What did he see, or not see, that the Stenographer got wrong – because she did get something wrong for him to call us back."

Logan spent the whole of the trip reassuring Catherine that everything was going to be ok and they would soon have all the answers to her questions.

Inside, Logan was as worried as Catherine, he just didn't voice his concerns because he knew they would compound hers and probably lead Catherine to panic.

Not that she wasn't doing a good job of doing exactly that even without his worries to add to her own.

"Ok, you need to calm down and steady your breathing," he told her when they pulled up in the hospital car park. "That's the way, slow and easy."

"Bloody hell, anyone would think I'm giving birth," Catherine snapped, her temper short due to the worry.

Reaching across to take her hands in his, Logan smiled and said, "I'm right here with you and I won't let anything happen that you don't want to happen. But I think it would be good to hear what the consultant has to say — don't you?"

Calmer, Catherine nodded and reigned in her fears — if there were anything wrong with Katy she didn't know how she would cope.

As a private patient, at Logan's insistence, Catherine was immediately taken through to see Mr Kersteven

"Mr and Mrs Sayers, nice to meet you," the consultant greeted them and indicated for them to take a seat.

Before anyone could get another word out, Catherine said, "What's this all about, did you find something wrong with our baby or what...what? She asked again, throwing her hands up in the air and letting them fall back into her lap.

Logan took her hand and gave it a gentle squeeze. "My wife is very worried about the pregnancy — though I've assured her it's probably just a confirmation check-up. Was I right?" Logan asked, watching the consultant for any sign of greater concern.

"You're exactly right," Mr Kersteven smiled. "Though it's probably just a blurred photograph, I wanted to check your dates myself, just to be sure."

"That's it?" Catherine asked, clearly sceptical.

"I promise you, it's no more complicated than that," Mr Kersteven assured them both. "I have everything set up in the next room, if you wouldn't mind going with the nurse she'll help you to get ready."

The nurse, who had stood quietly observing the conversation, now moved forward to indicate the way.

Catherine followed obediently, but looked back at Logan with a narrow eyed frown before the door closed between them.

"Now you can tell me what you didn't want to say in front of my wife," Logan told the consultant.

Sighing deeply, Mr Kersteven leaned back in his seat and weighed his words. "There is a shadow on the scan photographs that is causing me some concern," he said, towering his fingers and bringing them to his lips. "It is possible that it is simply a photographic anomaly and we can dismiss it after a second look."

"But you don't think so," Logan stated, his brown eyes penetrating as if to read the consultant's mind.

"No...I don't," Mr Kersteven admitted quietly. "Quite honestly, I'm not sure what the anomaly is – but it could be serious, that's why we need to check."

Christ, was he going to lose Catherine the way they'd lost his mother. One minute she'd been in fine health, then the cancer had been found and his mother had died very quickly – almost overnight, it seemed to Logan.

But he couldn't lose Catherine that way – he would do anything in his power to find a cure. No matter what it cost or where they had to go, he would not lose Catherine!

"If it turns out to be cancer-"

"Please, Mr Sayers, don't assume the worst – it may simply be a photographic shadow," Mr Kersteven insisted.

"But if it isn't, if it is cancer, would Catherine be able to commence treatment right away?" Logan asked, determined to get to the truth.

Mr Kersteven sighed again, this time heavily and with a sadness that was telling. "There would be a very difficult decision to be made, should that be the case. The pregnancy would not survive the treatment, I'm afraid."

And he'd been telling Catherine that this was just a routine check-up – what the hell would they do now?

"Let's go in," Mr Kersteven rose from his seat and

waved a hand towards the examination room. "There's no point in wild speculation – until I've examined your wife, that's all this is."

Before stepping into the room behind the consultant, Logan was careful to erase all signs of worry from his face.

"Where the hell have you been?" Catherine demanded, glaring from one man to the other.

"Just giving you time to get ready – preserving your dignity," Logan chuckled softly, and took Catherine's hand in his and gave her a wink.

"Huh, you've seen everything I've got in close-up, and he's about to so where's the dignity in that?!"

He couldn't stop the laughter that escaped him, but inside Logan was choking on his fear.

"Alright, Mrs Sayers, just bring your feet together and up to your bottom, then let your knees flop open," the consultant instructed.

Catherine closed her eyes, did as she was told then looked up at Logan. "See what I mean?" she frowned as the ultrasound probe was gently inserted.

For what seemed like endless moments, the screen showed all kinds of nothing that Catherine couldn't make out, but there seemed to be no sign of Katy.

"What's going on – why isn't the baby on the screen?" she asked anxiously.

"We'll get to the baby in just a moment," Mr

Kersteven assured her. "I'm just taking a look around the womb to make sure that everything is nice and healthy. Now..." he murmured after another moment or two, "...let's get a look at baby."

Catherine and Logan were glued to the screen, desperate to see their baby growing safe and sound.

"Well I never," the consultant frowned.

"What?" Logan asked, turning his gaze to look at the doctor. "What did you find?"

The consultant moved the probe and focused in more accurately then smiled," I found a second heartbeat – that must have been the shadow I saw – one embryo hiding behind the other, but only one heartbeat showing at the time."

"I don't understand..." Catherine looked from the monitor to the consultant, her super brain unable to translate anything she was being told "...two embryos...one heartbeat...what does that mean?"

But her mind was already racing ahead – Ellie, she had gotten pregnant with twins but only one of them had developed to the stage where she had a heartbeat.

The sadness was deep and profound, the sense of loss unbearable, and tears began a slow trickle down the side of her face.

"Mrs Sayers..." the consultant was trying to get her attention "...Mrs Sayers, there was only one heartbeat at the time of the first scan – there are two now," he smiled when Catherine focused on him again. "There are two very strong heartbeats showing now – you're going to have twins in around 32 weeks from now."

"Twins…" Catherine looked up at Logan her eyes wide and her mouth agape "…did he say twins?"

Logan was grinning from ear to ear, his eyes filled with relief and love and every emotion that came in between. He'd feared the worst and had been given the best news ever.

"Looks like we're going to have our hands full," he told her, then bent to kiss her soundly. "I love you so much – I can't tell you how much I love you right this second."

Not worried about the nurse or the consultant, Catherine flung her arms about Logan's neck and said, "Ellie, we found her."

Back in the consulting room, a few minutes later, Catherine and Logan were filled with questions.

"Did she do something wrong, the woman who did the first scan, or just not do it properly," Catherine asked.

"Neither," the consultant smiled confidently.

"Surely it has to be one or the other," Logan frowned.

"Not at all, but let me explain," Mr Kersteven said, holding a hand up when Catherine would have interrupted. "The first scan was very early on – right at the time when the embryo can develop a heartbeat. But it appears, your babies didn't develop at exactly the same rate – the second heartbeat just wasn't there to be detected yet."

Catherine and Logan looked at each other, deciding if the explanation was good enough, or right at all.

"I can sort of see what you mean…" Catherine turned back to Mr Kersteven, her head nodding thoughtfully "…but does that have implications for the one who developed slower than the first?"

Smiling broadly now, Mr Kersteven shook his head. "Absolutely not – no more so than if the hearts had begun beating at exactly the same time," he assured them. "In fact, we don't know that the second heartbeat didn't start the moment the scan was over – we just don't have a way to tell. But the fact is, both heartbeats are clear and strong – I have no further worries at this stage of the pregnancy."

When they got outside, Catherine and Logan looked at each other then he swept her up, twirling her around.

"Well, we've gone and done it now…" Logan grinned as he slid Catherine down his body to the ground and held her against him, "…it's definitely twins. I can't wait to spread the news."

"When I first found out I was pregnant, I would have been devastated to find out I was carrying twins again," Catherine told him, then her smile turned into a grin.

"Now, I couldn't be happier — Katy and Ellie, just as it should be."

"I think Ellie was trying to tell you that she was there, we just needed to look for her," Logan smiled, touching a hand to Catherine's cheek. "And now she's found, I'll bet your dreams will be a lot happier."

And they were. That night Catherine dreamed the same dream of Christmas with the boys and Katy, only now Ellie wasn't sitting in a corner all by herself, she was tearing open presents alongside her sister and the smile she gave Catherine was heart-warming and full of happiness.

*****

If you have enjoyed this book by Susan Elle, please leave a review at the point of purchase. Thank you.

Susan Elle